The Purple Duke
and
The Red Baron

D1737251

Denis De Luchi

FOR NOEL & CAROLE

DEDICATION

To the men who don't fly airplanes.

CONTENTS

ACKNOWLEDGMENTS

The inspiration for this book comes from all the empty headed people who think going to war is anything but the last possible option.

Chapter One

Who is the Good Guy

There are those mother's sons

We trundle off to war

In uniforms as amulets

Against the cannons' roar

Or give them tanks to ride in

And guns to point and shoot

And tell them they are heroes

When they're just low hanging fruit

Or, like me, some fools go off

Choosing airplanes as a ride

So when Death it comes acalling

There is no place to hide

A knight in aero-amour now

That's how I picture war

And when I bomb a mother

I think of her no more

It's all too ghoulish, too insane

But my leaders say it's right

One kills for god and country

And dreams demons every night

Last five stanzas of *Wash and Wear Fabrics for Light Brigade Horsemen,* an epic advertisement by Ralph Lauren. In it he wears spandex jodhpurs and a shiny nylon helmet. He is disarmingly modest as usual, with his sword sheathed and his pistol holstered.

I was born in 1831. Because of a DNA quirk, I can't grow old and die. I can be killed.

I start this episode in the Journal of My Life in:

November, 1914

***

I was a bit surprised. He should have lived in a better neighborhood. The street was narrow and dark, so I had a difficult time finding the house number given me by Sir Ronnell Regan, recently recalled ambassador to Serbia. Fortunately, it was a short row, so I could count the doors I passed, figuring an increase of four numbers per door. Number 120 should be about 30 doors down. I lit a match. 152. I went back a few doors and lit another match. 126. I was out of matches. I admonished myself for not bringing a torch. Then again, why would I? I went back two doors and felt the numbers. 120. There were no ground floor windows. Perhaps there was a dim light coming through a second floor window. The man was an ambassador for god's sake. A 'sir'. What was he doing in this shabby place?

I knocked and got my answer. The painted lady who answered looked me over and said, "What d'yew want?" I suppose Sherlock Holmes could have used her accent to locate her origin within a four block area. I just recognized it as being from the least desirable streets of London.

"I don't mean to bother you," I said. "I was told I might find a certain gentleman here." I withheld the name. I remembered how I met Sir Ronnell in the first place – outside a whorehouse in Istanbul. I presumed then, and continued the presumption, that he wouldn't use his real name in places like this.

"No one here but 'arry."

"Is 'arry tall, curly blonde thinning hair, well dressed?"

"I 'ave a lot of blokes like 'at."

"Well, I think this 'arry is the bloke I'm after. The one I'm supposed to meet here."

"This 'arry is my biznuzz. Meet summer else."

"Would you just tell 'arry that Damon is here?"

"Nawp. Git out now."

"I wasted two matches finding this damn place. It's that important. If you don't mind, I'll just tell him myself."

"Nawt on yer life." She stepped in front of me as I headed toward the stairs.

"Miss, I try never to harm a lady. I will therefore set you on your ass very gently if you don't get out of my way."

"Ya will, will ya?" She took a swipe at my face. I set her on her ass, not all that gently. She grunted when she hit the floor, then she shrieked.

From another room, probably the kitchen, I heard, "Ya avin' trouble ou there, Betsy?"

"This bloke 'ere wans t'see 'arry."

A door swung open, and a big fellow came barreling through. "'e duz, duz 'e."

It was a worse neighborhood than I had originally thought. I shuddered to think Betsy and her huge friend might even be pillars of this community. It was obvious they ran a small business with some efficiency. It was also obvious that the best treatment I could expect from the approaching officer of the guard was to be thrown out the front door. He would probably try to add a few injuries to the insult. However, at this point I had been a practitioner of Eastern martial arts for 65 years or so. As he reached out to grab me I poked the fingers of my right hand into his Adam's Apple, about up the first knuckle. He gurgled. I never did catch his name. Betsy shrieked again. I picked her up and smiled straight into her eyes. "Please, Betsy. Let me retain this self-delusion of mine – that I'm a gentleman. Just tell me where I can find Harry. You know – 'arry."

Betsy was trembling. Her eyes went to the stairs. "I know he's upstairs," I said. "I don't want to disturb other clients. Which door?"

"Ri at the top," she said.

I took the steps three at a time, which would be pretty good for an 82 year old man. Well, for any other 82 year old man. Since my physiology was a lot closer to 28 than 82, I was used to it. I flung open the door at the top of stairs, jumped through, and stopped at the foot of the bed. There was Sir Ronnell Regan, former Ambassador to Serbia, spread-eagled, limbs tied to the four bedposts, buck naked. A woman, who might have been Betsy's twin sister, stood near one side of the bed. She shrieked. She sounded just like Betsy, too. Only her clothes were different. She wasn't wearing any. Her only adornment was a small whip in her right hand. Sir Ronnell, with some aplomb, said, "I'd hoped this reunion would be a bit more formal."

I took a deep breath. "I only understand about half of this," I said   "Your sex life is your business. If you needed spectators, I wish you had chosen someone else. I would have preferred to attend a Gilbert and Sullivan play for entertainment myself. So, why am I here? Is this involuntary? Am I saving your bacon once again?"

"No, no. You just arrived too soon." He turned to the woman. "Yorkshire pudding, Aileen. The fun's over for now."

"Yorkshire pudding?"

"My safety code." He relaxed as Aileen untied his limbs. She even smiled at me.

What does one say when a woman wearing nothing but a small whip gives one a bright smile? "We need a little privacy now, Aileen." She nodded at me, still smiling, and started for the door. Before she closed it behind her I said, "Please tell whoever the fellow downstairs is that I didn't mean him great harm. If he's conscious, that is."

"'is nym is 'enry," she said. Still friendly, I noted. I noted one other thing about her. She was an honest woman. The hair on her privates matched the hair on her head.

I turned back to Sir Ronnell, who was unhurriedly getting dressed. "You must have had a reason for wanting to meet here. If you are ashamed of me, we could have met at a nice quiet pub someplace. Spared me all the naked bodies and odd equipment."

"As I said, you're too efficient. You got here sooner than I planned. I should have been downstairs waiting for you."

"Why in this place at all? Any place else would have been....better?"

"Not really. No one but a few trusted servants know I come here. One of them smuggles me out of my house through the back entrance. Every place else I go I'm either followed or preceded by observers."

"But what's that all about?"

"Good heavens, man, think about it. A Serbian starts a war on my watch. If I'm not incompetent or corrupt, I'm a double agent. Oh, no one says as much, and I get brandy at my club, but the suspicion is all around. And you. You're a poison apple. The Hapsburgs have complained to England about you, since they got you from George, and everyone thinks you had something to do with the assassination." He was pulling on his socks, so he was starting to look like a former ambassador. I still had the image of a naked old man bound to bed posters, but it was beginning to fade. He continued.   "I'm glad you remained unseen and contacted me privately, and I'm glad you changed your name."

"Alan Roderick was the name I was born with. I have all the official documents to prove that, although for reasons we'll leave unsaid, the birthdate has been changed. I'm officially twenty eight."

He did a little calculating. "That would make you an infant when we first met in Istanbul. I think you overdid it."

"That between you and me. No one else has that history with me."

"I'll admit, you look that age. How do you do it?"

"Meditation. I spend long periods in such deep thought that my cells hibernate." When he looked as if he actually believed that, and was probably going to get into some Fountain of Youth nonsense, I put the conversation back on point. "So, we were both in need of a safe place to meet, and this is it. The question is, what should I do now?"

"Answer just one question for me. Actually two."

"Ask."

"Have you made up your mind which side you're on, and if it's England's, are you willing to risk your life for this country?"

"Yes. And yes."

"So, that means you no longer feel allegiance to the Hapsburgs, and your love affair with the Turkish woman is over?"

"The Hapsburgs are fools, and that beautiful woman was two loves ago. Women and I are destined for passion, but no permanency."

"I envy you that. You discovered tonight, if you didn't know already, how I express my passion with women."

"To each his own. I don't judge."

"Yes, you do. You just seem to know what's really important and what's just human dawdling. You overlook my sins, but consider the Hapsburgs a blight on the world."

"Well, in the end they did me no favors. After all I tried to do for them. But that's history. It's the clouds on the horizon we must deal with now."

"And that's exactly why I wanted to meet with you."

"So, here I am, in your favorite whorehouse, ready to save the King."

Sir Ronnell was dressed. He went to the door, opened it and yelled down the stairs, "Aileen, could you bring up a bottle of brandy? And two glasses. And my friend wants to know how Henry is."

There was a pause and then Aileen, in almost a shriek, answered, "Be ri up, Yorksher man. 'enry's breathing again. Can't seem to speak very well, though."

Sir Ronnell turned to me. "At least you didn't kill him. I would have been persona non grata if you had. You don't know how hard it is to establish yourself in a place like this. I'm one of the family, you know. They're very discreet about me."

"I'd rather not know the details of your relationships here. I am glad Henry's going to be all right. I certainly didn't intend to kill him."

"Well, let's get down to business. If you're as good as I think you are, the power crowd will be grateful to me for recommending you. I'll be done with the nasty rumors about me, and you'll be a valued citizen again. We'll be past the past."

"Recommending me for what?"

"That I don't know. It's a special project, and the person I'm sending you to didn't give the details. Wouldn't. Couldn't. I still on the outs, you see. But it's risky and it's important, and that makes it right up your alley."

"Who is this person?"

"Brigadier General Sir David Carlyle. Head of the Royal Flying Corps."

"Does this have to do with aeroplanes?"

"It may. Have you ever flown one?"

"Of course not."

"Doesn't matter. If that's what it's about, you'll be taught to fly."

"That's comforting. Not just 'Here's your mission, there's your mode of travel, that little lever makes it go' kind of thing."

"No. That's not a worry. The main problem is getting a meeting in the first place. It won't be in a place like this, but it will be even more secretive. Just you and Sir David. With guards outside, of course. If you both like what is said, you have a job. For King and country."

"So, how will I be informed about the time and place?"

"Take a room above the pub Billy and Ewe. You know where that is, I'm sure. A message will be delivered to you there."

"Suppose their rooms are all taken?"

"I have one reserved for you."

Somehow I knew he would say that. I swallowed my brandy in one gulp and stood to go. I said to Sir Ronnell, "This didn't take long. You might want to get back into your chains again. Pick up where you left off. Aileen looked like she was just getting warmed up. I'll just go make amends with Henry, and you'll be one big happy family again."

Denis De Luchi

Chapter Two

I wonder about living forever

You got to exhilarate the auricle

And defibrillate the ventricle

And exuberate the metrical

And don't mess with spirits in between

Cause when you inebriate the oracle

And defoliate the virginal

You alleviate the magical

And wind up with nothing in between

Swami Karawandachandrashekar offered these words of wisdom as he walked across the Blue Nile on the backs of crocodiles.

The neighborhood Brigadier Sir David Carlyle brought me to was the antithesis of urban squalor. The houses were at least a mile apart, so one would have to go many miles to find one that housed whores. Lusty farm maids maybe, but no whores. The car Sir David had sent to whisk me away from the Billy and Ewe, unmarked and with a civilian driver, turned into a lane bordered by holly oaks, a lane that led directly and at great length, to a two story stone house. The grounds were immaculate, with well-tended garden; even some topiary. The stone façade was clean and the windows were clear, even though each revealed nothing but closed drapes. One could see the drapes really well. There was a guard at the front door, and this made me notice two others, each at a front corner of the building.

The driver, who hadn't said a word to me during the trip from London drove right to the door, stopped, got out, and opened my door. He was still wordless.

The guard at the door wasn't. "Name?"

"Alan Roderick."

"That's correct."

"I know."

"Password."

"I don't know any password. Actually, I probably know an infinite number of them, but that's the same as not knowing any, isn't it?"

"Wait here."

He disappeared into the house, and in a moment a tall man in military uniform, replete with shoulder strap, shiny belt, collar trinkets and a weaponless holster came to the door. He looked me up and down, and may have had bemused thoughts about my own dress. That would only be fair. He said, "Sir Ronnell said you should recall a password. Think back to where you were last with him, and him mentioning a safety code."

It amused me think that a naked whore knew the secret password too. "Yorkshire pudding," I said.

"Very good," General Carlyle replied.

"I believe Sir Ronnell wanted me to check on you. Can you describe the circumstance in which I received the code?"

Sir David a bit surprised, but shrugged. "Over brandy at his club, of course."

"Very good." I simply loved the English upper class of that era. The world for them was: a bunch of colonies (one of them upstart), the continent of Europe, the British Isles, England, and, at the head of it all, striving mightily to keep it all steered in the right direction, the Lords and Ladies. You didn't tell Whitehall your fantasies. It had its own.

Sir David led me into a cozy parlor and motioned to a plush armchair. I sat. Without asking he went to a stand, poured a stiff dose of brandy into a tumbler, and handed it to me. He took a chair directly opposite me. "I've had my brandy for the day, so don't wait for a toast." After I took a swallow, he said, "Have you any idea why the head of the Royal Flying Corps would want to meet you in a country house?"

I took another swallow. It was good brandy. "I hope it's because you're about to offer me a job flying airplanes." I said this without emotion. I really did hope that, but anything David Carlyle wanted would at least be interesting, and probably dangerous. I needed both, and my gut warmed to thought that I was about to be offered both. My luck seemed to be holding. I added, "I will tell you from the start that I'm game for just about anything."

"Do you have loyalty to England? Are you willing to lay your life on the line, in places where there will be no comrades to back you up, no government wall to hide behind?"

"Let's put it this way. The war is a stupid idea, and will get worse. But the Germans are more stupid than the British – in fact, unforgivably stupid. In addition, I harbor an animosity toward the Habsburgs. The French

I don't care about one way or another. I have no idea what the Italians are up to. I'm not ashamed to admit that, because I don't think they know either."

"You are quite opinionated. How do you feel about the Turks?"

"That's more complicated. A woman of whom I'm very fond is sure a war will set back Turkey's quest for democracy. She and I worked hard to prevent this war just for that reason. In retrospect, I think she and her group are wrong. The downfall of the Ottomans will be expedited, so a war may aid her cause. That would please me. I know that if Turkey becomes preoccupied with internal problems, England and France will have freer rein in the Middle East. I'm not sure that's such a good thing, but I really don't care. All this, although futile, is inevitable. As a Scotsman by birth, I can claim loyalty to the King and to England in time of conflict. If I say I am on your side my honor dictates that I remain on your side, until you demonstrate you no longer want that commitment."

"Well, I trust Sir Ronnell's judgment. And I believe that the tales of your escapades in Serbia are true. You seem a man without a country until you decide to adopt one. You have adopted England as I see it."

I took yet another slug of brandy, draining the glass. He noticed that, fetched the decanter, and filled the glass. It was not a sophisticated use of brandy, but it would save him trips to the bar. I asked, "Just what have I adopted. Will there be aeroplanes involved?"

"Yes." He paused and leaned forward, elbow on knee, hand to chin. "Do recall your English history. Letters of Marque and privateers and all that?"

"Quite well."

"You see, I am certain that airplanes will play an important role the war. There will be more than artillery scouting and communication advantages. There will be air battles, and grenades thrown into encampments from airplanes. Most of this will be overt, but some," and now he leaned even closer, "will be done by individuals, a lone man in an airplane, seeking targets of opportunity, spying, choosing his own routes and activities, anything to disrupt enemy planning, anything to strike at enemy morale and confidence. There are no rules for this person, no time constraints. He can strike in the dark, at Sunday worship services, wherever he chooses. If he can't hit a target with his hand held bomb, or if the target if too large, he can land and do what needs to be done before he escapes back into the air. If he lives, no one knows what he has accomplished. If he dies, he dies alone, and still no one knows. What I'm describing is a thankless job, but one I believe will be crucial to the outcome of this, as you put it, stupid war."

"If that's a job offer, when do I start?"

Now he leaned back. "We can start your flight training immediately."

"Where do I report?"

"You're there."

***

I sent for the few things I had left at the Billy and Ewe. I always traveled through life with as few impediments as possible. If one lives, as I have, for nearly 200 years, and keeps accumulating crap, he will reach a point wherein he is no longer able to breath, for the weight of his impedimenta. How did Abraham carry around the shekels he used to buy Jerusalem? Careful analysis shows he couldn't. My guess is he gave up a few concubines and his third son, Islamabad. If one isn't going to buy Jerusalem, one only needs a few clothes and a lot of greenbacks, or these days, a credit card. Maybe Abraham had a Visa.

Brigadier Sir David Carlyle thought he was giving me pause for thought when he told me of the dangers and loneliness of the proposed service into which I was about to enter. He did, but not the thoughts he imagined. For a person who knows he has a greater probability of living hundreds if not thousands of years, the thought of physical danger becomes more and more attractive as the years pile up. In 1914 I was already 81 years old and wondering how much longer I really wished to carry on. Now, at over 180, I realize – I can't do this shit forever. Even then I had vowed to myself never to fall in love again. Of course, I have made and broken that vow many times since then. I just can't help it.

So, on that country estate in Wiltshire, even as I started training to become the Phantom Pilot of the Royal Flying Service, I fell in love three times in one day.

The first love was a big, black Irishman (I wondered if his ancestor was with mine in the Spanish Armada). He was a pilot and mechanic and my flight instructor. I loved him from his first words to me: "Ye'll either floy loyk yer part o th' 'plane or oil kill ye meself." Rusty O'Doul.

The second love was the plane. The Avro 504. Most Englishmen who learned to fly learned in the Avro, rotary engine and all. I will stop trying to imitate Rusty's accent, since it is tedious. His assessment of the Avro was: "She has ton-feet of torque, but she's forgiving and if you caress her she'll do anything you ask. She's not a lady. She's a lusty woman."

The third was, and by this time it should be predictable, a woman. Nancy Wright was assigned to be my record keeper, aide, cook, confidant, and … probably nothing more, at least as far as Sir David was concerned. He had chosen her, I'm sure, because she was bright, closed-mouth, and a little homely. It took me just two days of frequent conversations and interactions with her to realize she had a very fine figure and more importantly one of the most beautiful souls I have ever encountered. She was very much a lady and, it turned out, a very lusty woman.

I really liked that flight school.

***

"So tell me, Rusty. Why do you think of an airplane as a woman?"

"They're just like women. All different, and all the same. They're too hot in the summer, too cold in the winter, and they get naughty on you when you least expect it. You're taking a chance every time you get in one. Give 'em plenty of love and they'll take you far. Fly 'em wrong and you wind up as flaming wreckage. You tell me the difference." It sounded like poetry in his brogue.

"Ah, Rusty. Hard to argue, but I see it differently. I see airplanes as the armor and steed of a knight. You don't get in them, you put them on. If you do, you'd better have the skills to make it all work. The skills of a pilot, the skills of a warrior, the skills of a priest. You're donning the suit of a demigod, and you be giving either benediction or doom to those you encounter."

Rusty could only smile. "With my metaphor you only need to be a lover. According to you, you have to be Perseus." He squinted at me. "If you're going to try to ride Pegasus, you'd better be a natural pilot."

***

It turned out I was. After my first ride with Rusty he hardly had to touch the stick at all. He showed me a maneuver, I did it. On the first day I could land three points, two points, or one point in a cross wind. I could ground loop and take off downwind. On the second day I could do all the aerobatics he was ready to teach, and created one or two myself. In fact, I may have done an Immelmann before Max himself. A lot of people think he didn't do it first anyway. It was one of those things. I was doing a loop and a 'what if' came to me. Why not roll out on top? If you don't know what I'm talking about, Google Max Immelmann sometime. Anyway, I was as surprised as Rusty at how quickly I took to the concepts of flying, and the employment thereof. I was in fact a natural. I don't think I would be a natural astronaut, though. Bottled up in a capsule for months, pissing in my pants during an eight hour spacewalk – it takes a special person. It's not me.

Rusty did suggest a bunch of tricks in case I ever got into a hassle with an enemy pilot. I'll go into those later.

***

My love affair with Nancy Wright was inevitable. When I wasn't flying or talking flying with Rusty O'Doul I was sharing, nay creating, my life with Nancy. She was responsible for making me official and yet non-existent. This would have been difficult for someone who was otherwise normal, with a public history. It was somewhat more difficult for a man who was fresh-faced recruit but who was over eighty years old.

From the first session she had tried to hide her reservations about me, but reservations don't hide well behind a blatantly skeptical expression. I couldn't blame her for that.

"You realize," she said, "that all we know about you is anecdotal. Things Sir Ronnell Regan has told us, things on wanted circulars from the Habsburgs. You have some papers created by them, things you told them to record, but there is no official witness to any of the details. For instance, when were you born?"

"How old do I look?"

"Mid-twenties."

"Then I must have been born around 1890." I couldn't tell her I had bribed an official from Invereagle to place a birth record for Alan Roderick in a baptistery file in Edinburgh. I forgot which date it currently had, since I changed it every so often. My distillery in Invereagle was now the biggest employer in town, so I got pretty much what I wanted. It's just that I couldn't ever remember the exact date on the last update. Maybe I never knew them in the first place, since I didn't care that much. I had, without trying, become the truly existential man, which meant I could never adopt the philosophy of existentialism. I leave it to the reader to figure out why that is so. Enough bullshit.

"What date in 1890?"

"Pick one."

"April 1st."

"Good."

"Where?"

"Edinburgh."

"Parents."

"Dead."

"I mean, names."

"Roderick."

"First names."

"I don't know. Jack and Jill."

"That's not helpful."

"Nancy, you're creating my story. So, be creative."

"But for the official records…."

"Be creative."

"So, for the hidden files of the Royal Flying Service, you want your identity to be Alan Roderick, with whatever details I make up about your life?"

"That's right."

"Can you at least give an education background?"

"I attended Edinburgh Academy."

"Really?"

"That much is true." I didn't tell her when.

"So, how will you be known to the enemy, or anyone who hears about whatever exploits you perform. Sir David seems to think you're some sort of hidden force. I'm going to be keeping track of you, explaining whatever you do to whomever is important enough to need such briefing. What shall I call you for such briefings? Mister Magic Hero?"

Her sarcasm hurt. I told her so. "Don't think I sought this mission. I just want to do what I can in a war I tried my best to prevent. Yes, there is something personal here, but mainly I just need to do something useful. I'd rather be a scientist, but I can't seem to sit still long enough, so I'm stuck do this kind of adolescent activity. Don't hold that against me. I can't help it. That's the way things have worked out for me, and you should know better than anyone involved here: if there are any heroics, no one will ever know it was me. And that's the way I want it."

The skeptical expression had disappeared. "You know what? I believe you. You do things like this because you can't help yourself. And you really don't want glory and medals. You want to remain a cipher. I don't quite understand. You probably don't, either."

"Not quite is an understatement. I do know that, for reasons I won't go into, I need to remain a cipher. My bona fides are anecdotal, word of mouth. People either believe what they hear or they don't. I go on, either way."

"You're an interesting fellow." As she said that, with lips pursed, she became less homely. In fact, her lips were quite attractive.

***

Our intimacy started abruptly, as a lovely surprise. She had called me to her quarters to do our daily chronicling of my sensations and experiences in learning to manipulate airplanes and their accoutrements with expertise. I arrived early. I knocked. No answer. I knocked again. Still no answer. I opened the door. Her little parlor was empty. I could hear noise from her bedroom, so I took a chair.

She emerged from her bedroom naked. She started when she saw me, then seemed to relax. "Well, that can't be undone now, can it?"

We had spent so much time together, had learned so much about each other, that there seemed to be no need for either of us to be embarrassed. If she was at ease I should avoid a fuss also. "No, it can't," I said. "And I can't honestly say I'm sorry."

"Not sorry? This body isn't exactly an artist's dream. My breasts are small and my hips are fat."

"Well, Reubens wouldn't have used you for a model, but I've never been crazy about his women anyway. Botticelli would have loved to have you when he was creating Birth of Venus. And she's as good as they come. Although you're not popping out of a sea shell."

She laughed the magical woman laugh. "Enough talk about my naked body. Let me cover up and we can get down to work.

So that's the way it was with Nancy and me. She had climbed inside my mind, found out as much as I would ever tell anyone, created a new identity for me, and eventually poured out her heart to me. This last took a great deal of scotch whiskey to shake loose, although she never got incoherently drunk. She wasn't much more than a hundred pounds. I'll bet she could drink most men twice her weight under the table. She only demonstrated that ability twice, though, and mostly settled demurely for a glass of wine or two. It wasn't the whiskey that made her my soul mate. It was her desire.

As I have said, she wasn't a ravishing beauty. Her nose might have been considered a little large, her eyes were not engaging, her lips a bit remarkable. It was her laugh that drew me beneath the skin, where I found a glowing soul. And it was her skin, when I saw her naked, that also contained a nearly perfect woman's body, the kind that would have made pre-historic Homo Sapiens males decide that mating with this female was a good idea. Her body and soul did that for me, and when I finally let her have her way with me I knew it was one of the best decisions I ever made.

***

The next morning, Rusty and I had our way with the little Avro. It was great fun and more importantly made me feel even more strongly about the invincibility of a good airplane with me in it. After we landed, I had to remark to Rusty, "There, my friend, is the difference between airplanes and women."

"And that is..."

"With an airplane you're the boss. That's the only way it works. With women, it's better to let them drive."

Rusty O'Doul grinned. "I thought you might be getting cozy with Miss Nancy. I'm glad to see it. Nary a word to Sir David."

Denis De Luchi

Chapter Three

Enter the Purple Duke

Oh I had a lady in Wiltshire

And I had a lady in Reims

And I had a lady in London

But none were the girl of my dreams

No she was a lady in Stillson

She lived on a very nice farm

I thought it nice to romance her

It surely could do her no harm

She turned no heads when she passed men

There was no glamorous flair

But she had a woman's persona

And a soul as light as the air

So I kissed her and held her and told her

Things she was anxious to hear

And when time and love wrapped around us

I thought there was nothing to fear

But as always my exit was certain

And the blanket of love came apart

I left her there crying in anger

I left her with half of my heart

This is an old Aleutian ballad, sung by seal hunters to calm Aleutian grizzly bears. It was made famous by the American singer Jo Stafford under the title *Shrimp Boats is A-comin'*.

"You can't be serious," she said.

"Why not?"

"The Purple Duke? You want your code name to be The Purple Duke?"

"Why not? After the first intercepted dispatch, the name Purple Duke will strike fear in the hearts of the enemy."

"More likely they will laugh themselves into incompetency. That might work for you."

"Just run it by Sir David. If he approves, The Purple Duke will be instrumental in the fall of Kaiser Wilhelm."

"Well, just in case he does, you'd better go practice being intimidating. You're not naturally very good at it, you know."

"I haven't managed to make you tremble?"

"Not from fear."

"I'll go practice then."

"See you for dinner."

***

We had rehearsed dry up to this point, me in my lovely Avro, Rusty in a Bristol Scout he had managed to borrow. We fought quite a few fights over that farm, fights Nancy witnessed. She told me she finally had to quit watching when it dawned on her that after the play came guns. Forward firing guns. Guns with intent to kill, maybe not the pilot, but to get a 'kill.' The concept of air superiority was incipient, if not yet in the military vocabulary.

Today was to be my first day with weapons. When I saw the preparation Rusty made, in the airplane and on the ground, I gave my silent thanks once again to Sir David for providing me with this aeronautical genius as a mentor. Rusty placed a Lewis machine gun on the wing just above the cockpit, strapped to a sliding mount. It fired just to the right of the propeller, and the gun could be pulled back and canted down for reloading. I had two sideboards for safe stowage of reload drums. I had fired the gun on the ground, and learned how to shorten bursts, to be more effective with less ammunition. At the rate of fire of the Lewis, one could use up all the ammunition he could carry in less than thirty seconds. Modern movie goers might count more than six shots out of a six shooter, but they aren't aware that the hero with the automatic weapon couldn't possibly keep blazing away on one clip of ammunition. If he holds the trigger down, his first burst is his last.

"Remember," Rusty said. "These targets I've laid out around the farm are stationary. Don't let the temptation to completely destroy any one of them take over your mind. I want to see holes in every one of them, not all your bullets in one mangled one. Approach each of them differently – out of a roll, in a dive, at almost a stall, from an impossible angle. Get fancy. You have the skill. I'll be watching from the house. Nancy will be in the cellar."

"You know we positioned the targets so I won't be shooting toward the house."

"It isn't that. She just doesn't want to think about you and shooting airplanes."

"She's known all along what we're here for."

"You're not stupid. You have to see that she romanticized the whole thing at the start. Now that gun barrels are heating up fast, she's forced into reality."

Now I needed Rusty's help in one last thing, a thing I couldn't explain. Like all my romances, this one had to end. I needed Nancy to accept me going off to war and possibly getting killed therein. In fact, I was planning on living through the thing but being officially killed anyway. Killed in action is cleaner for a woman, She needn't wait and hope. I have tried my way out many times, "I truly love you but I have to get on down the road. Can't tell you why." They never believe that. A situation in which I might actually be killed is ideal. When the word comes to her, she believes it. So I said, "Rusty, you have to convince her to watch. It's best for her, and for that matter it's part of her job. She works for Carlylr. She needs to back you up on your report to him. She needs to be honest with herself and her duty. All that shit. Please do that."

Rusty grinned, just a small, reserved grin. "So, you're going to end a love affair, and you haven't the guts to do it straight up."

"That's because I don't want to end it. I wish it could last a lifetime. There are reasons beyond my control that make that impossible. It has to do with that 'lifetime' phrase. Rusty, I can't explain it. You have to trust me on this. It has to go down with me not coming back to her. If you're thinking I have a wife and kids in Scotland, think that. Just think of what's best for Nancy.

The grin, slim anyway, faded to nothing. "Okay. But I tell you, outside of this job, this work, I don't know what to make of you. You seem like a decent fellow, an honest man, but strange. That's what I call it. Strange."

"Rusty, I'm even strange to myself."

***

The live firing exercise was as much fun as I expected. Neither the Avro nor the Lewis let me down. I made the pass on the first target straight on. This was the first time I had used an airplane to aim a gun, and this was a nimble airplane and a very rapid firing gun. I passed directly over the house on a straight line for the target, which looked very much like those set up for archery. I framed the target in the rectangular gun sight in the windshield. It was at first just a dot, gradually increasing in size. I kept it centered. There were wire reticles in the rectangle, allowing me to judge distance if I knew the approximate size of the target. I was looking for about 200 meters, where my line of sight would converge with the stream of bullets. I fired a short burst before that distance. I saw puffs of dirt just below the object. Just what I expected. The next burst blew pieces of wood, straw, and painted material out of its back. It appeared to have a hole very close to its center. Rusty had mounted the Lewis perfectly.

It was time to experiment, to have fun, to see what sort of mischief the three of us, me, the Avro, and the Lewis, could make. I came at the next target from the side. When it was just about abeam I made a hard ninety degree turn into it. I believe that airplane could turn with a wing tip touching a pylon. Looking down the nose I could see the next prize just a little to the starboard. A little left rudder, a burst, and the target nearly disintegrated.

I went full throttle and pulled the Avro up until she started to shudder. I was high and gaining airspeed as I approached the next objective. As it came abeam I started a loop. A half roll put the target under my belly as I went vertical. As I came screaming down from the loop the target passed over my head and gradually came down into my gun sight. The engine was winding up, even with the throttle in idle, but I had to keep the nose down. I had a lot of altitude on the dummy enemy. I fired the last of the rounds in the canister. The enemy died.

I leveled off, pulled the Lewis to me, and changed drums. I next wanted to see what happened when I fired the Lewis with the airplane near stall speed.   I gained a comfortable altitude and throttled back. I was a safe distance from our test grounds, so I could fire straight ahead. I held the altitude until the stick got sloppy and the plane hinted at a shudder. I fired away on the Lewis, a good long burst, using most of the drum. It only took about four seconds of continuous fire for the nose to fall, disregarding my efforts to hold it up. The Lewis had stalled her out. I let up on the trigger and let the airplane regain flying speed. I would have to think more about air battles at very low speeds.

There and then, however, it was time for more insanity. I changed drums again. I selected the target we had placed on a little knob, the highest point on the property. I swung toward it and rolled inverted. Could I successfully aim the Lewis when I was upside down?

Why not? It should make no difference to the Avro, that little angel who just loved to fly. Would the mechanism in the Lewis know the difference? I was about to find out. I centered the target in the sight. The reticles told me it was about the right distance. I shot a burst. I was high. I hadn't accounted for the change in attack angle when inverted. I let the nose down a little, which started me toward the ground, to which I was already too close. I fired. One burst. One more. I saw bits come off the target. I did it. In fact, I over did it. I had concentrated so much and pushed so hard, I was on the target before I realized it. I pushed the stick forward to get the nose up. Too late. I wiped out what was left of the target with my vertical stabilizer, the part of the tail that holds the rudder. That I didn't mind. I did mind the fact that the target wiped out my vertical stabilizer, and all the shooting had left me near stall, upside down and rudderless. I yelled 'Shit!" loudly enough to scare the horses. Just before the Avro stopped flying I managed to roll upright. My friend the throttle made all ninety horsepower answer my call. With elevator and ailerons I had enough control to make a safe landing, although the plane was a little skiddish (yes, skiddish, not skittish) on the way back. I plopped the Avro as near to the house as possible. The stabilizer was Rusty's problem, although I would watch him repair it, in case I ever had to do it myself. As the engine spun to a stop, I said, "Damn." I still had a canister of ammo left.

***

Rusty had come running with his après dinner brandy still in his hand. He didn't carry on too much about the vertical stabilizer; just enough to impress Nancy how much I was past just 'bold' as a pilot. I don't know if the aphorism "There are old pilots and there are bold pilots but there are no old, bold pilots" had been coined yet, but Rusty had said something like pilots as crazy as I had no longevity. He was a friend.

Nancy was putting the dishes away, so she talked over her shoulder. I don't think she wanted to look at me. "He's probably right, you know." The big plates went into the cupboard. "You don't seem have any reasonable fear of death." Dessert plates went in. "Why should the rest of us have anything to do with you? Tea cups were next. They took a little longer, so I let the question hang there moment.

"You probably shouldn't. Rusty has no choice. It's his job to get me ready. It's Sir David's job to try to win the war with people like me. It's my job to take risks. You should just do your job, which is to keep track of me, up until the time I go off to whatever I'm going off to. I can't think of any justification for you caring more than that."

She turned. Her eyes were red. "It's not that simple and you know it. I care for you more than just taking care of you. I suppose it's love. Am I supposed

44

to deny myself that?"

"That's the eternal question, isn't it? From my point of view, women are, for the most part, superior beings. But they have this Achilles Heel. They love. It's what saved the human race, for what it's worth. Oh, I've loved too, but I think I've killed more people than I've loved. That's not good, and it preys on me. It makes me want to go to war and see if I can get it out of my system. The hair of the dog. And if I get killed in the process – well, that's my Karma."

"Oh, shut up. Don't talk like that. Your job is to try to win the war, to end the war, to stop the killing, and you know it."

"That's a better way to look at it. I'm not adverse to that. One way or another, though, I have to go do it. And to do it with good results, I'll have to do some crazy things."

She sank into a chair and sighed. "I know. You have to do what they picked just you to do. And I'm left to wait and worry and try to lose myself in my work. Unless you can tell me you don't care for me. Never did. I was just a convenience. Look me in the eyes and tell me that."

So, I could lie and deliberately destroy her self-worth, or be honest and let a letter from the Royal Flying Service bring tragic news to a noble woman with fond if painful memories. Honesty is the best policy.

Except when it isn't. I said, absolutely truthfully. "I can't do that. I love you and I think you've felt that from the first time we came together...If you love me you'll let this discussion end, and never bring it up again. It's war, and we both have our parts to play."

She got up, came to me, caressed me, sought my lips with hers, then leaned back. She cupped my cheeks hands that felt like angel's feathers and said, "We've probably talked enough as it is." She led me toward her bedroom.

***

We made love off and on for almost two days. As my assistant, my accountant, my record keeper, my cook, and my cheerleader, she had been efficient, exuberant, and nearly flawless. As my lover, she was tender and enveloping. When a woman has made you turn off all your alarms, she is free to steal in and take possession of your body and soul. Nancy did this with such grace I would have begged for the theft. I abandoned all my cautions about loving and being loving. I was going to war, to an unknown fate, and we both accepted that. There was only the moment.

When the letter came we accepted that, too. Brigadier Sir David Carlyle wanted me on the earliest possible train to Lincolnshire. He would meet me in Lincoln. My next step toward the front would follow. Nancy read the letter, lowered the hand holding it to her side, and said, quite flatly, "It doesn't mention me."

"I'm sure he has work for you elsewhere."

"I'm sure. It doesn't mention Rusty."

"Rusty will be somewhere in France, fixing airplanes."

"Yes." Her gaze was distant. "Yes," she said again, very softly. "And you. You just disappear from my life."

"I'll write. If I can. When I can. What I can."

"Can we say goodbye right here, right now?"

"Is that what you want?"

"Yes. I couldn't stand having you close and knowing we have to part. I need to get the parting over with."

"I understand." I reached to embrace her but she pushed my arms back. She kissed me then, without the embrace, a kiss so tender but so filled with love it burned my lips. "I love you too", I said.

She went into her room and closed the door.

Denis De Luchi

Chapter Four

The Purple Duke Rides

You're cast upon a sea

A sea of guts and glory

You leave behind the things you hold so dear

You set your little sails

You start your little story

You gird your loins against the things you fear

The wind is at your back

The tide is running rough

The weather is so bright and crisp and clear

But as you tack to port

The sail starts to luff

And the slapping of the waves is all you hear

And as you slip adrift

You begin to ponder

Why does it all appear so very queer

And in the end you know

You didn't have to wander

For what you needed had been truly near

A rondo sung in four part harmony by the Squint family of Freeport, Kansas, during their annual okra harvest.

She sat there in the middle of a mowed field on that little farm beside Glaston Priory. Sir David glowed, as if showing me his newborn child. It was solid purple, nose to tail, except for some black markings that looked much like the Habsburg griffins. These were on the tops of the upper wings and the sides of the fuselage, just forward of the tail. "Isn't she a beauty?" he asked. "Had her painted and marked myself."

"What is it?" I had to ask, since I hadn't seen or heard about this airplane before.

"In production, next year, they'll be called Nieuport 17's. But this is special. Note that bottom wings are only half as wide as the tops. In the production models these will be a little weak. That limits the dive speed but decreases the drag and weight. They might break in a dive if the pilot isn't careful. This one has stronger spars in them. A little extra weight, so we added more power. The standard engine has 130 horsepower. This has 150."

"How did you do that? And why not do it for all being built?"

"It's too complicated for production. For the higher RPM the timing mechanism is like a Swiss watch. And the weight of the bracing for the spars plays havoc with the balance. The thing is just barely dynamically stable. Only a superior pilot can make it behave. She's the royal purple, and she's only for the Duke." He glowed even more when he said this. So Brigadier Carlyle had had a brat, and I was going to be the baby sitter.

Worse. An urchin left in a basket on my doorstep, since the first thing I noticed was the single cockpit. "I'm obviously going to have to teach myself to fly this admittedly almost impossible to fly airplane."

"The aeronaut who brought her here did just that. Surely you won't allow him to be a better pilot than you."

"Don't you find it a bit ironic that you spent all this time and trouble and money to get me ready to terrorize the Hun, and I might kill myself in this machine right here in England, on my first attempt at flight?"

"I was always willing to take that risk."

"You're a courageous leader, Sir David."

The sarcasm wasn't lost on him, but he didn't seem to mind. He just said, "I really do know what I'm doing."

I could only smile at that. He really did know me.

***

I started the takeoff roll. The torque pull to the left was much greater than the Avro, but I expected that. What surprised me was how easily the airplane came off the ground. It had so much weight forward, between the engine and reinforcing spars and buttresses, that I was planning to haul it off by sheer strength and will. The ferry pilot told me it wanted to fly, but I didn't believe him until the very moment it leaped into the air. Sir David had mentioned a small change in the design and pitch of the horizontal stabilizer. (The little wings on the tail.) Non-aeronauts think the wings of an airplane hold up the front, and the little wings in the rear hold up the back. That's not true. The little wings in the back hold *down* the back. Of course, this only applies to older airplanes. In the twenty first century aeronautical engineers screw around with everything. In 1915 it took all their screwing around just to make something that actually managed controlled flight.

The powerful engine made this little angel truly homesick. It reached for the sky with little effort on my part. I wasn't about to lose vigilance, though, after all the warnings about possible instability. This machine and I were projected to go far together, and right then I was still over the Glaston Priory pasture. I wanted to stay close to that pasture while I tried a few tricks.

I climbed, put it into a left spin, recovered easily, climbed, spun to the right, recovered easily, climbed, and started aerobatics. A few rolls, a loop, combinations of loops and rolls designed to change direction precisely ninety or one hundred eighty or not at all, hanging on the prop, hammerhead stalls to both sides – all these things were easy. Any underlying insttability didn't seem to want to surface. Was I that good? I couldn't make this lady be naughty. It was she who was seducing me.

I looked at the Vickers Automatic, mounted and synchronized to fire through the propeller. It would be the next thing tested, but that was for another flight. Turning back toward the pasture, I wondered if the Nieuport would be as easy to land as it was to fly. It was. When I pulled the throttle back on that big Gnome engine, I stopped flying. I bumped through the cow turds to a stop.

Sir David was there to meet me. He had with him a fat, disheveled man, sweaty even in the cool morning. The man had close set eyes, a drooping black mustache, and a ponderous gut. The beady eyes weren't looking at me. Just the airplane. They rolled over the machine, trained momentarily on every strut, every surface inch, on the wheels, the control surfaces, the windshield, the Vickers gun. I felt as if I were in combat, as if an enemy pilot was shooting at me. I could hear the thwack of bullets, the ripping of fabric, a ping off the propeller, wood chips flying from the struts. I looked for my blood on the floor of the cockpit. Unlike my Vickers, the beady eyes seem to have an infinite supply of bullets. This was my first taste of combat. Sir David was oblivious to the battle. He merely said, "Some ship, eh?" To my nod, he turned to his hefty companion. "Alan, I want you to meet your ground school. This is Maurice Leplombe. He's the man who redesigned this

Nieuport to make it your special machine. He's going to teach you everything about it."

This pig farmer? As I climbed down from the cockpit I put out my hand and said, as warmly as I could, "I'm so pleased to meet you. This is a fine airplane." He grunted as I shook his damp hand.

Sir David was in a hurry. "I'll let you two get acquainted," he said, practically over his shoulder. I thought he also said something about an urgent meeting, but he was walking away when he started the next sentence, and it was truncated by the closing of his car door.

I looked quizzically at Leplombe. He shrugged and said, "He's shagging his driver. It's a cushy job for her, and she's a handy shag for him."

"And you know this how?"

"The driver is my sister-in-law. She lives with my wife's mother. She's just full of details. Apparently she and the Sir take turns spanking each other. They use various mechanical devices for various things. Exchange sexes and that sort of thing. And they do a lot with their mouths. Flossie – that's the driver - laughs about the size of his organ. Says she's in no danger of choking."

I got the image of the very formal Brigadier Sir David, his trousers around his ankles, his knobby knees to the floor, performing cunnilingus, with his bristly gray mustache causing a rash in a sensitive area. It was replaced by the image of Sir Ronnell Regan tied to bedposts by a Limehouse whore. "I guess," I said, "it's a requirement in England to be knighted before you can have imaginative sex. But you've told me more than I want to know about that Sir David. From now on, let's just gossip about the purple airplane."

Leplombe snorted. I decided I wanted as little conversation with this pig farmer and his pornographic memory as possible.

***

I had always prided myself on my ability to size up people quickly and accurately. In the case of Maurice Leplombe, I was completely wrong. It turned out that he only talked dirty because he wanted to put me at ease. In reality, he was a brilliant man in what would become the discipline of aeronautical engineering. I remember one of my first conversations with him.

"The airplane seems to fly just fine. Sir David warned me that it might be unstable. It might try to get away from me."

"It was very unstable when I first modified it. You don't want to know how many times it crashed."

"Crashed? How can that be? How many have you had to build?"

"Just the one. I've put it back together just a little differently each time. I've modified every surface, every brace, every strut. Sometimes I've worked several days straight through, setting an example for my crew, for my pilots."

"Your pilots. And how many have you lost through these crashes?"

"Thankfully, there have been no deaths, although a couple of men have given up flying. Involuntarily."

"But you've had no trouble getting people into that cockpit?"

"Did you balk?"

"I didn't have a choice. Besides, I didn't know about all the crashes."

"You have to remember, aeronautics is a new science. We don't have hypotheses. We have wild ideas. We don't have carefully designed experiments. We have trial and error. Sir David heard about the trials and the errors. He wasn't completely up to date. I'm giving you an airplane which I think is, right now, the best in the world. At least, as a weapon of air war. I believe it will do whatever you ask of it, and I expect you to ask a lot. I know you've had some training in aircraft repair and maintenance. I'm going to give you a lot more."

During that period I actually moved into a spare room of the cottage occupied by Leplombe and his wife Clara. Clara's sister Flossie came to dinner several times. In my presence she never spoke of Sir David and fancy fucking.

***

My sweet little Avro wasn't through with its service to me. They flew it up so it could be of great use once again. This time it was to tow targets, so I could get used to shooting the Vickers gun at moving objects. "Remember, unless you can fly straightaway on the enemy's tail, you must pull lead. Have you experience at shooting airborne fowl?" Sir David was being patronizing.

I answered, "A little. I have more experience at shooting running men." This may or may not have been true, but it shut him up. I just wanted to climb into the Nieuport and blow the flying target to pieces with the Vickers.

I was disappointed Rusty hadn't come with the Avro. We trusted each other explicitly, and mutual trust was handy for pilots towing targets and pilots shooting at them. The fellow assigned to fly the Avro was not yet out of his teens. I'm not sure if he understood that people can be killed when bullets are flying about. He had an American accent and a bit of a grin when he said, 'I'll hold her steady for you, sir."

I had to get used to the 'sir' shit, since I had been appointed a Captain by Sir David. I told him I probably couldn't act like a Captain, since I had no idea what being a Captain entailed. He said, "That's not your problem. It's just for record keeping, and to give you authority to get what you need in strange places. In fact, let's make you a major. That will be more impressive when you claim priority for petrol or ammunition in at a field manned by the French. Or even the British." So I got my first promotion before I even started, by claiming I didn't know what I was doing. War is such a strange endeavor. Military tradition is subverted by the drive to kill the enemy.

Actually, I didn't give it much more thought than that. I hopped into the Nieuport, soared into the sky, and blazed away at the target from every possible angle, excepting those that might hit the teenager in the Avro, and from every possible attitude. It was much easier to nail that target upside down when my vertical stabilizer wasn't nearly scraping the ground. I landed, refueled, and restocked ammunition several times that day. The Avro pilot had to land several times also. He needed gas. And he needed new targets. I had shredded all he towed. I humbly submit, I was that good.

After I proved to everyone, myself especially, that I could make my special Niewport, designed by trial and error, do anything I needed, and probably some things I hadn't even thought of yet, I made my last landing at Glaston Priory. I taxied straight toward the figures of Sir David Carlyle and Maurice Leplombe. To their expectant looks I said, "Let's take this machine to war."

Sir David was suddenly sober. He patted Leplombe on the shoulder and nodded toward the car. As Maurice trundled off, I realized I was alone with the Commander of the Royal Flying Corps. This wasn't the man who engaged in kinky sex with Flossie the driver, or the man who beamed at the birth of a wicked airplane, or the man who had risked his reputation on a stranger with reputed martial skills, recommended by a man who engaged in even kinkier sex. This was the Commander of the Royal Flying Corps. He said, "Make your goodbyes tonight. If you want to write notes of farewell to anyone who might care, I'll see that they are delivered. Leave the envelopes unsealed. As a final precaution, I won't give you your orders until you are ready to take off tomorrow. Enjoy your last evening in England for an unspecified but probably long time."

What could I say in that thoroughly expected moment? "I understand."

***

Dinner with the Leplombes was quiet. They knew I was leaving in the morning and I think they were truly sad. I thanked the god I didn't believe in that Flossie wasn't there. Even though she avoided pornographic gossip around me, her conversation was still banal. My feelings for Leplombe were anything but banal, and I managed to express them after dinner.

"Maurice, it may be only the opinion of a non-expert like me, but I believe you must be the best airplane builder in the world. If I feel any trepidation about what I must do with your creation, it has nothing to do with the creation itself. Thank you for giving me the very best machine possible."

"You know," he said, "I didn't build it with you in mind, not consciously. But somehow that's exactly how it turned out. I made it for a man like you. May it serve you well, and all the way to the end."

I bade them goodnight, and went to my room to write two notes.

My note to Rusty was simple.

My dear friend and mentor, Rusty

By the time you get this, I will be some place on the other side of the Channel. We may never meet again. Please know that any success I might have in this mission is due directly to you. If I fail, it will be my failing. I wish you a long and happy life. Maybe I'll have the same. With all my gratitude,

Alan

I resorted to a different syntax for Nancy. I wrote her a poem.

My Dearest Nancy

Here is how I think of you.

I never love you as much

As when you wake up in the morning

Without the false armor of makeup

Your hair its wild self

Your lips naked and inviting

Your eyes wide at the wonder of another day

Your smile the freshest and most honest thing on earth

You're an image that can't be captured

Some old Italian painters tried

Some younger Dutch guys tried

Some even younger Frenchmen tried

I know where they were going

But they never quite got there

Every man who has loved a woman gets there

In the head, in the heart, in the gut

If only for a fleeting moment

So I take that image with me, to run through my head every day   And so it will, until we meet again.

Alan

I put the notes in envelopes, leaving them unsealed as directed. I would give them to Sir David in the morning.

Chapter Five

The Purple Duke Rides

I've crossed the Channel many times

In every vessel made

At night, at dawn, in Summer's sun

In cliffs of Dover shade

I've thought about it many times

The men who've come and gone

Are not remembered by the sea

As waves wash on and on

And so it has to be with me

I'm just a speck of dust

To be forgotten by the sea

Just doing what I must

A talking seagull whispered this in the ear of William the Conqueror.

***

   Sir David was pensive, but not grim. It was a war, people were getting killed, and there was no need to dwell on tragedy. Men in war make a silent agreement on that. Everyone loses something in a war; victor or vanquished. Everyone leaves a bit of their humanity on the field. Sir David and I were now in business together. He traded envelopes with me. My two were unsealed; the single folder he handed me wasn't. He stayed my hand when I started to open it. "Let me give you a sense of the orders before you look at the details. Your destination today is a farm in Belgium. It is a little south of Bastogne, and actually behind German lines. It's close to a Ninth Century castle, somewhat in ruins, but a place to hide petrol and ammunition for your missions. There is a large scale map of the farm in the envelope, showing the arrangement of the farm buildings, which is unique in that part of Belgium. You'll notice T-shaped dairy barns on either side of the house. Coming from the South, the left one is actually a hangar. Once you spot the castle, you should have no trouble finding the farm. You can follow rail lines out of France, and what is left of them into Belgium, but it is up to your airmanship to find the place and land quickly. You don't want to be spotted by the enemy lingering over your redoubt, and the place is unmarked except by the layout I've mentioned. You will find credentials in the folder so that the people at the farm will accept and aid you. If you leave quickly you will have plenty of daylight to make a successful trip."

"I take it there are orders in here to dictate what I'm expected to accomplish."

"Yes. In short, you begin by disrupting rail transport. There is a marshaling yard just across the German border. It is an important distribution point for supplies to the front. You will harass these trains with that Vickers. You might even try dropping grenades on the engines. It would take skill and luck to make such a thing work, but I know you have skill and Regan tells you have more than your share of luck. At any rate, you'll know you've done a good job when they divert planes from the battlefield to come and confront the mad train wrecker. Then you become an air-to-air combatant. You should go ahead and keep wrecking trains between air battles."

"On my time off may I toddle on down to Vienna to romance the Archduchess Gisela? I owe her a little tenderness, since everyone thinks I was the cause of her public humiliation."

"That episode has been buried by the war. But, if you find a few free moments, you're welcome to start an affair."

"How will we communicate, you and I?"

"Couriers. Delivery boys. We have a cadre of people who will smuggle supplies. But you will be the entire escadrille south of Bastogne. The commander, the chief pilot, the head mechanic...everything but the mess sergeant. You'll be the Royal Flying Corps there and you'll be on your own."

"I understand. Is there any other mission?"

"No. Just do it. I hope we meet again someday, Major."

"Au revoir, then, General." I waved a kind of salute as I climbed aboard the purple machine.

***

I had hoped to see the sun glistening off the choppy waters of that moat called the English Channel. This was my first crossing in an airplane, and I had imagined thousands of moving mirrors, all changing angles and patterns, shooting specks of benign sunlight at me. I should have known better, the probability for a gray day being much greater than for a brilliant one. That part of Europe is best captured in black and white. Nature imagined the coasts of France and England when she was colorblind. She gave us a gray sea, gray white cliffs, gray tidal flats, muddy gray waves. She later, by virtue of occasional sunny days, came up with a greenish sea and green trees. She needed us to provide wars so that she could use her red tones in the blood on the beaches. She had her way with me that day, though, for I flew all the way to Bastogne above and below the gray. Oh, there were occasional earth tones on the battle fields, but Nature had nothing to do with those.

I navigated by pilotage, as Sir David had suggested, following rail lines into Belgium. They remained in good repair, so the Germans must have been industrious in the their maintenance. That, or no one was attacking the rail system yet. I would soon take away that second option.

I had an expected time of arrival for the ruined castle that was to be my home. It popped into my windscreen pretty much to the minute. This didn't surprise me. Yes, I'm lucky, but that is the kind of luck one makes by careful planning, and, I must admit, good guessing at the expected winds. When I circled to head for the farm I patted the plane and thought fondly of Maurice Leplombe. The modified Gnome engine hadn't even hiccupped once, and the only noise the rest of the craft made was that heavenly music of wind through struts. I could fly this Nieuport anywhere there was a little air to breathe.

There it was, the farm with the two dairy barns. I fixed on the left one, pulled the nose up and started a roll to left. I kept climbing, into a kind of loop, let the nose drop through the horizon and pulled back on the throttle. As I came down out of the loop, I was aimed a little right of the left barn, just a small turn. I slipped the airplane from one side to the other to rid myself of altitude. I came across the pasture fence aimed directly at the barn/hangar, touched down, and continued to bounce across the field. I could see two men rolling aside the hangar doors. The purple airplane was my calling card.

***

The doors closed behind me as the engine wound to a stop. Before I even unstrapped a man was on the wing. He was a tall, thin fellow, with a long, thin mustache. I handed him my bona fides. He glanced at them, at me, and at the purple airplane. He said, in Belgian French, "Welcome, Major Duke."

I spoke enough French to buy absinthe in a bistro, so I would get by. I hadn't yet thought of myself as 'Major Duke', but that was fine. That's the way they thought of me, and that's what I'd be. "Just call me Duke," I said. I thought of the real duke I had assassinated less than two years before. I shouldn't have to pay that price, since I wasn't really a duke. I was a major. I should go with Major. But I wasn't really that, either. I was just a guy with a purple airplane. A damn good purple airplane. That was my commission and royal lineage. I was the scion of Sir David Carlyle and Maurice Leplombe. It was unlikely parentage, so really, these folks could call me what they wished. "Call me Duke. Call me Major. Call me comrade. Whatever you like."

"I'm Henry," he said. "And everyone will think of you as Duke." He jumped off the wing as I climbed out of the cockpit and indicated his approaching comrade. "This is Louis."

On Ree and Louie. That's all I would ever call these men. I suppose those were their real names. It didn't matter. I was The Duke. That's all they ever called me. On Ree, Louie, and Le Duc. We had a good working relationship while it lasted, which wasn't meant to be that long. How long could they be expected to hide a purple airplane, behind German lines, once I got started blowing up freight trains? That wasn't my main consideration at that moment. "Comrades," I said, "I'm tired and hungry."

"You can stay here tonight," Henry said, "but you'll be safer in Chateau Violet from now on. You probably saw it as you approached. It's less than a kilometer from here and we've prepared living quarters. Well hidden, of course."

At first I thought he was kidding me. The Purple Castle? I would go along. "I suppose it belonged to the

Purple Duke."

"Yes. Charles Pompignon. In the Eleventh Century. He was called the Purple Duke."

He wasn't kidding. "And he got that name because he was a great warrior and his armor was purple?

"No. Because his skin was purple. We know now it was a blood disorder. At the time, people thought it was too much wine."

"So you want me to live in a place called the Purple Castle, where the Purple Duke once lived, and leave the calling cards of the Purple Duke when I start blowing up locomotives, and you think that's a good hiding place for me? That it's not the first place the Germans will look?"

"We feel certain they will think it would be the last choice for the modern Purple Duke's hiding place. So it will be the last place they look."

"I'm too tired to argue."

***

They were lousy cooks, and their own quarters were a smelly, abominable mess, so I was glad I wouldn't be rooming with them. I was too used to Nancy, who had pampered me, fed me well, and kept me organized. Her memory was incentive to take good care of myself. It would be hard, though, since my own dwelling had everything but a neon sign announcing my presence. Purple Joe's. No cover. Happy Hour every Friday. I could only hope the Germans were smart enough not to notice the obvious.

I learned about the cooking disability of On Ree and Louie that first night. Henry said they had prepared their very best recipe for my welcome supper. Louis' special ratatouille. It was a vegetable stew, alright, but it tasted like the main ingredient was moose shit. Don't ask how I know what moose shit tastes like. In a very long life like mine, with many desperate situations built in, one does many things to survive. You'd be surprised how satisfying fried moose shit can be on the frozen tundra in Alaska. On a French farm though, served with a tolerable red wine, it's just horrible.

So the wine was okay, the ratatouille made one want to run in any direction away from the pot in which it was made, and the rat's nest of a house made a renovated dungeon in a ruined castle seem like a dream home. "Thanks for the dinner. I guess I'll get along to bed. I want to start hunting for troop or munitions trains at first light." They showed me to a damp alcove, one with a slightly stronger, even more unpleasant smell that the main hall. I wondered: when they renovated a room in the castle, did they import the stink to make it feel like home? Please. No.

Breakfast was some sort of Dickensian gruel. It was nourishing enough, I guess, to see me through the day. After choking down as much as I could, I let my two erstwhile cohorts help me aim the Nieuport out the doors of the barn. I kicked the wheels and checked the oil. The controls were free, the Vickers loaded, with extra ammo belts in the cockpit pockets. I had my issue Webley, and two quick load cylinders, eighteen shots in all. I was ready.

We cranked the engine and it spun up instantly, another tribute to Leplombe. I turned my beautiful machine into the wind, gave a small wave of goodbye, and I was thumping across the pasture. Some cows were already out. They were unperturbed. They didn't run and I didn't hit any. And, yes, I was wearing a scarf. I had two scarves; one purple, one white. I thought the white contrasted better with the purple airplane, so it was the one trailing on that, my first takeoff into real aerial combat. I knew something about going into battle, and I was by that point in my life inured to distracting emotions. Still, on this particular takeoff, I was excited.

I headed east for the German marshaling yard. The day was brilliant; the greens and yellows of the countryside were fresh from Van Gogh's palette, playful and sweet and full of life, contrasting with the previous day's flight, which was am ink sketch by Durer. Before long I could see the puffs of smoke, tiny and distant at first, that signaled steam engines tugging loads around.

I headed a little south of the main concentration of puffs. The multitude of rails would then converge to my left, becoming a single line that ran not far from my castle home. It would be tempting to let the trains come to me, but that would give the Huns a bead on my whereabouts. No, I needed to do a little extra flying, to make them think I was coming from someplace else. Even with this precaution, I didn't think my relationship with On Ree and Louie was meant to last. In my orders Sir David had provided me with an alternate station, although no mention of a new mission was contained therein. I couldn't worry about that right then, however. I was in an airplane, in proximity of enemy logistic routes, and in possession of the means to disrupt them. That's all there was in that moment.

And in that moment I spotted my first target. A locomotive with a long line of freight cars was just approaching the western end of the yard. The tracks had narrowed from fifteen or twenty sets to about three, all heading toward a single line, outbound to the front. There was no hurry, since I wanted to debilitate the train on the single track, and I wanted to check for ammunition cars. I was told they would be unmarked, closed, and somewhere in the middle of the train, appearing unguarded and innocuous. I could make out several such cars, all about in the middle of the line. I decided to make the sure bet. One couldn't miss the engine.

I rolled to my left, lined up on the puffing monster and pushed the nose down to put it in my gunsight. When it filled the reticle, that big black very hot cigar heard the Vickers talk. I fired longer bursts than I had planned, but I was so fascinated by the puffs of direct hits on the boiler superstructure and the escaping vents of steam that I didn't want to let up on the trigger at all. I pulled over the engine at the last second, did a Chandelle, and came back for an attack from the other side. I ran the gun out of ammo, flew over the train, and flew to parallel it in the opposite direction of travel. Was the train slowing?

Most pilots couldn't reload a machine gun belt in flight. One had to lean out over the windshield, flying with the stick between his legs. It was a reckless procedure, and by that time in my life I loved reckless procedures. By the time I a mile past the train's end I had rearmed the gun. The train was definitely stopping, if not stopped already. I passed back directly over it, passing along and firing at the cars I thought might contain explosives. Nothing exciting happened with them, although by now a few people were shooting back at me. I felt a few thumps, saw a few tears in the fabric of my wings. They didn't trouble me. I was coming up on the engine.

It was completely stopped, right where I wanted it, on the main line with no spur nearby. I fired a few bullets for good measure, continued west while I loaded the last of the ammo belts, and turned to make one more pass along the train. I saved the bursts for the cars that might be high value cargo, and even threw a few grenades, which missed miserably. I didn't allow for trail, something I would have to remember. I was out of things with which to make mischief, but I had one train to my credit. There were a few souls still shooting at me as I headed away to the south, my pretended destination.

***

I knew I couldn't live with On Ree and Louie. I was already calling them the Smelly Brothers although their real surname Smilloux. I also knew I needed their skill and dedication to live at all. After I had taxied my purple plane into the cowbarn/hangar, they immediately set to work. They patched the bullet holes with amazing speed, help me check the engine and gun, greased the wheel axles, smoothed the prop blades, and, most amazing of all, rolled the airplane onto a wooden platform, which they raised with two block and tackles and many tugs to a place above the lost. They put the thing out of sight, on a table that passed for the top of the barn. They had taken to Leplombe's highly modified engine, and assured me they would keep it running if I couldn't. When we were through putting the purple bird to bed I had to squeeze through a screen of guilt when I told them I was anxious to get to my own quarters. The guilt grew when they told me they had stocked my dungeon with foodstuffs and wood for the stove and would help me carry my belongings as they accompanied me there for my first entrance. The only thing that kept me from hugging them was that they smelled as bad as the rest of their house.

***

It was a nice enough room as dungeons go. A cot, a small table, a kerosene lantern, a stove with a stovepipe leading out. Cooking would be a challenge. I fired up the stove that first night, knowing I could only use it at night, and possibly not at all. I would have to see if any smoke hung around the supposedly abandoned castle in the morning. But there were some foodstuffs and a few bottles of wine. On Ree and Louie were taking care of me. That left me to take care of business.

Chapter Six

The Bastardization of Purple

Of all the art you've ever seen, Ah

study the Rape of Proserpina

Note the texture of her flesh

Gaze as Pluto's hands enmesh

Bernini felt the grace depart

The maid gave body, never heart

And in the underworld that night

There was no beauty, only blight

Like Hades and Persephone

Or like a Wagner symphony

When royal purple turns to red

You're left with only blood instead

From *Playground Tennis,* by Helen Wills Moody, Chapter 2, The Backhand. Harpers Press, 1927.

***

It took the Germans ten days to understand I wasn't a random phenomenon. During that time I terrorized the rail yard. I'm confident I decommissioned at least one train a day, most times catching them after they had reached single track. I picked on the locomotives. I may have been lucky on an ammunition car just once, but I can't be certain. There was a boxcar sputtering as I departed one day, and I heard a great explosion behind me, although only a plume was visible on the horizon when I turned to look back. No matter. I stopped a lot of people and things from getting to the front, and that Vickers gun never jammed or misfired once. I went through all the petrol and bullets Sir David's couriers could smuggle to the dairy farm of On Ree and Louie. I also received a message. I was causing concern among the Hun generals.

That concern materialized on the eleventh day. I had tried to vary my arrival times at the yard to preclude some routine pattern, but I was constrained by having to arrive there in daylight and by having to be at the cow farm before complete darkness. So one day, when I arrived at my target, the Eindecker monoplane was waiting. It was their best combat airplane at that time, and it probably had one of their best pilots. His mission was obvious; eliminate the pest. I felt goosebumps, and perhaps a hint of fear, the fear of uncertainty. I had been in gun fights before, but never in gun fights between two airplanes. Did I know enough? Had I practiced enough? Was this the Black Knight who never lost a joust? Or was I the Black Knight who had never had one? That all passed quickly. I remembered my mantra about going to war. Do it in an airplane. That's as close to Do or Die as one can get. That's all I asked for.

I was surprised at how short the battle was. He approached me head on, so I could see when his own gun fired. Either he underestimated me or overestimated his own skill, but he started firing too soon. I pulled up and to the left, then immediately back to the right. He had tried to follow but was now slightly behind in the turns. By the time I was inverted he was off to my right instead of behind me. I turned into him. He thought I was going to ram him and turned away. Now I was on his tail. He turned, but not very hard, still underestimating me. I pulled harder on the stick, enough to get a lead on him. I fired a burst, then another. He leveled out and I fired a third burst. This last tore shreds around the cockpit. The Eindecker drifted off on a wing and began to loss altitude. I fired one more burst, straight on. The airplane seemed to break apart, piece by piece, as if some giant hand were deconstructing it. I couldn't bring myself to shoot anymore. In fact, I couldn't bring myself to shoot at a train, although I had gas and bullets left for a few passes. I felt sad suddenly, and I didn't know why at the time. I do now, of course. It's a question of two knights, engaged in mortal combat with each other, because that's what knights do. And neither knows

***

I suppose a bunch of people on the ground watched the air battle. Therefore, the German High Command, maybe a bunch of Prussian generals in Potsdam, got multiple accounts of the purple airplane killing the Eindecker. This would turn a few simple maneuvers by an unknown and therefore underestimated pilot into the daring and intricate conquest of a German ace. A reputation, perhaps a notoriety, was incipient, hung around the neck of whoever flew that damn purple plane. I figured I was a good pilot, but that kill was nothing remarkable. Still, I was sure those Prussian generals were making it so.

The net result for me was just one day free from air opposition, a day passed by German flight strategists in planning my destruction, a day passed by me shooting up trains at will. I packed all the bullets the Nieuport would lift that day, plus a few grenades. I brought three quick load cylinders for my Webley hand gun, and after I had shot up a few locomotives and thrown the grenades at likely munitions cars, after I could feed the beast that was the Vickers machine gun no more, I made one last pass, firing my Webly at anything that moved. I just wanted to piss the bastards off. I took a few hits; something even nicked my gun hand, drawing a few drops of blood. I wagged my wings to show them I didn't care.

***

I went out the next day armed to the teeth once again, on the off chance that I would own the sky over the marshaling yard for another day. I was wrong. There were two Eindeckers and a bi-wing Fokker awaiting me. I tried to imagine the strategists calculating the probability of my demise. I threw in the best pilots, the best airplanes, my demonstrated skill, their experience, and the certainty that there was only one purple airplane, only one persistent problem. They would go all out on the one objective. No distractions. No loss of focus. They were over their own territory, there would be no other air activity, gunners on the ground would aid them, and I had done a hell of a lot of damage already. Perhaps I had killed a few young lads. Maybe more than a few. The Purple Scourge had to go. I could feel their excitement, feel their anger. And just for the fun of it, I ran the numbers in my head. They had calculated a greater than 99% chance of success. A certainty. And they were coming at me, again head on, but now three instead of one.

If this were fiction I would describe undertaking an absolutely brilliant series of maneuvers that culminated in the destruction of all three enemy airplanes. But, you see, when I calculated their probability of success it included several scenarios, only one of which lead to the 99% figure. In that one, I chose to stay and fight. In one that lowered their chance of success to well below 50%, I ran away. I would obviously go with that latter, while making them believe, as long as I could, I was foolish enough to go with the former.

They didn't break apart as we closed on each other. That meant that while one or two might do the shooting, there was going to be a ram attempt also, probably by the bi-plane. They weren't going to break apart right away, to come at me from all sides. That made it easy for me. I was sure the Nieuport, with an engine they couldn't know about, would outperform them. I just wanted one last lick from the Vickers.

I ran the modified engine to its full power and even a little more. I wanted to gain airspeed for my escape. Closer. Closer. The middle airplane, the bi-plane, fired a burst. It was too soon, by about a second. I held fast and they did too. I fired immediately after their first shot, just to let them know I was in the game. I think I actually hit something, but that was of no matter. The two Eindeckers actually did break right and left to surround me, while the center piece head straight on. When we were as close as I dared, and I saw the bi-plane start to waver, perhaps lowering his nose a little, I pulled the stick back and began a rapid climb, straight ahead. The bi-plane sailed under me. The Eindeckers were still turning away, and I was dumping everything I could over the side. I threw out all the ammo cans, all the grenades, my map case, anything I could grab. Had there been dirty laundry that would have gone also. Every pound counted, as did every bit of horsepower. The throttle was hard against its forward stop, and my sweet purple plane was climbing like the proverbial homesick angel. By the time the enemy pilots realized what had happened, they had no hope of catching me. They couldn't out-perform me in any case, and now I had several thousand feet of altitude on them. When I leveled and the airspeed started to build again, I was faster than they. They could only watch me fly away.

To this day I wonder at the irony of my emotions over my first air battles. After my first victory I felt a sadness. After my first retreat I felt an exhilaration. What kind of warrior is that?

***

Back at the cow barn, On Ree and Louie and I cleaned and tuned the the Nieuport. After I watched them run it up to its hiding place, it was time. I had to tell them and it was going to be hard. They were proud of their work and were looking forward to a grand supper. I took solace in the fact that their grand suppers were basically pig swill, although they did have some good wine on hand. I would have to eat with them that night, which was a kind of penance for being the purveyor of sad news.

"You look serious." On Ree was the first to notice.

"I am." I hesitated only briefly. "Come, my friends. Sit down for a second. Relax. Let's pour a little wine." There was always a bottle handy. When we all had our cups I spoke,   rather bluntly, in my halting French. "Henry. Louis. This will be our farewell dinner." I let that sink in.

"What do you mean?" Louie asked.

"Today. What happened today. The Germans made it clear, with three airplanes, that they don't want me disrupting their rail activities anymore. I got away clean this time, but whether I show up there again or not, they will be looking for me. It does the cause no good if I stay hidden here for some undetermined period, and eventually they'll come searching around here. I have to be closer to that yard than the nearest French airfields, and I can't be hiding off in the old Holy Roman haunts, so it narrows down to some place close to the front in France or someplace in Belgium. They have to know I'm not flying from the front, because by now everyone knows the purple airplane. This is the most likely region for its base, and they'll be around soon. You can't hide that airplane up there if someone really searches this barn. And if they tear through the castle, they'll find someone has been living there. No. You have to go back to being just dairy men. I have to get that airplane out of here first thing in the morning. I want to leave no traces of it or me, just to protect you fellows. You can still be useful in the war effort. For me to keep being useful, I have to not get caught. At least, not on the ground. If they want me, they'll have to shoot me down. I won't give in any other way. But I will tell you this, so you'll know I'm human. I ran away today, because I couldn't win. I lived to fight another day, trite as it sounds. I won't quit, and you shouldn't either, but it's quits for us if I stay here. Do you understand?"

On Ree nodded. Louie said, "But it seems like we were just getting started."

"We fought a battle. They don't last forever anyway. Now we move on to the next battle."

"Where will you go?" On Ree asked.

"Better you don't know. Starting tomorrow, you never heard of me or a purple airplane."

"That will be hard," Louie said. "I've come to love that Nieuport. And I like you a little, too." I thought I could detect a glisten in his eyes.

***

We cleaned out my little dungeon in the Chateau Violet. There might be traces of long gone vagrants, but nothing of the Purple Duke. The Purple Duke. He wasn't really known yet; just the purple airplane. We would see about that.

I would carry what few belongings I had on the morrow's flight. I brought them to the cottage of the Smelly Boys. I could stand one last night there, although the gloom was stronger than the smell. On Ree and Louie had found a calling, a cause, and they believed it was flying away with me in the morning. We ate the stuff they called stew, drank a lot of wine, and I did my best to be a cheer leader. They got a little drunk and seemed to be listening to what I was saying. You still have a mission. You can do espionage. Sabotage. Arbitrage. Bird watching of the stiff winged kind. Train spotting. People peeping. Message transmission. Make butter spiked with rat poison for German troops. Use your imagination. Never give up. Never get down. Never….. I didn't know I had it in me. I had never been much of a cheer leader. I had always preferred to keep my own counsel, to steel myself and let others chose their own spinal metals. But I felt for these two Belgians. They needed to know there was more to their cause than the Purple Duke. That from the Purple Duke himself.

***

Still, they were gruff and reticent when they loaded

me into the plane. I hadn't dissuaded them their resignation. They felt the war was over for them; win or lose, they were destined to be spectators. Their ticket to making a difference was climbing into a purple Nieuport. I made one last try.

"Now, listen carefully to final instructions the courier brought. Headquarters wants you to maintain traffic with RFC and Ground Corps. If I encounter certain emergency situations I may return here for safety. You should be prepared. And you may be tasked further by other fliers, or even ground personnel. Stay ready. Keep this place as a safe haven and a base of operations." I was going to carry on with this line, but I wanted them to use some imagination. Let them provide their own meaning to what I had said. Of course, I was dissembling, but future events in a war are unpredictable anyway, so maybe I wasn't too far off. If there were any justice in the universe, Sir David wouldn't completely forget about these fellows just because I was no longer there.

They kicked over the prop for me, and I got a couple of 'bon voyages' from a couple of brave faces.

I navigated out the way I navigated in – via the railroads. Those tracks were so good to me, and I had been so hard on their trains. But I wasn't headed far. There was another little farm, much like the one I had just left, in the Champagne Region, outside the town of St. Chalon. That was the next private airfield of the

Purple Duke. There I would graduate from combat with locomotives to combat with airplanes. I was as exhilarated as the Smelly Boys were depressed.

Chapter Seven

The Terror of the Skies?

I try to reconstruct

The man that I was

Or the man that I might have been

But I was what I was

And I wasn't what I wasn't

And for me that ain't no sin

Graffito found on the center left column of the Brandenburg Gate.

Mons. Poindex was as French as a Notre Dame gargoyle. In fact, when he spoke one could imagine the cry of an angry church demon, beseeching any listener to hurry up and do it. 'It" could be anything, from a milkmaid using all four teats in the proper order to a mechanic tightening a bolt just so. I didn't mind his mannerisms, since he was the crew chief of my own private airfield, and he ran it well. He was well dressed, immaculate, and although quite thin, commanding. He wore a Salvador Dali mustache, although that's a retrospective observation, since I hadn't heard of Dali at that time. I liked the entire situation much more than my dungeon and hayloft arrangement at the other milk farm. It was a safe retreat, and everyone at St. Chalon was clean and free of offensive odors. Mons. Poindex was adamant about bathing, and they all used that rough peasant soap made from lye, lard, and lavender. Knowing, as I did, that I would be using my skin for a very long time, I tried not to throw it away needlessly on such soap. I used plain water, although I made a pretense of scrubbing with the bars.

On this farm I was free from the clandestine activities required when one is operating behind enemy lines. Here I could relax a bit, so I took two full days off to get used to the place before I began my assigned duties. The food was good and the wine was better. Mons. Poindex had no wife (through the not uncommon death-during-childbirth of his third daughter) but a good housekeeper and cook. His three daughters were tolerably good-looking, but something told me to forego any thoughts of romance, so I was nothing more than polite to all three of them. After two days, I was aching for a fight.

Poindex had my airplane ready to go almost from the moment I arrived. He had a good mechanic and easy access to materials and supplies. Apparently his liaison with Sir David, through the French High Command, gave him a certain amount of power, usually available only to generals, and sometimes not even to them. That, of course, put the onus on me, because I was the reason this dairy farmer/field commander had so much pull. Even the French were counting on me to do something extraordinary. Me, I just wanted to rat race with the German pilots.

***

Intelligence dispatches told me the best place to find aerial opponents was near the trench lines, not far from us. Near was the key word. There was a certain no-man's land of trenches, open graves that alternated between the opposing forces, and the air battles were fought on either side of this zone. I would go hunting there, and I would have to be careful. At this, my first foray into the actual war zone, I was still unknown to friendly pilots. There was no reason to think they would take my purple plane to heart until they saw me shoot down a Hun.

The first morning out I didn't have to go far.
Before I even reached what one could call The Front, I
encountered a flight of three huge aircraft. I could later
learn they were test models of the Gotha bomber, a
German heavy, meant for warfare against urban and
industrial areas. I further didn't know that these were
out for a test drive, perhaps to bomb anything that
looked bombable. Because of their size and their
enclosed crew cabin, they looked formidable.
Formidable was what I wanted, formidable with the
Black Maltese Cross emblazoned on fuselage. I readied
the Vickers.

I took the lead airplane straight away. My usual
luck came into play, since this was the best tactic for
these particular airplanes. They weren't particularly
nimble, and they didn't have a forward firing gun readily
available. I took out the big engine with one burst and
rolled onto my back to escape collision with the dying
airplane. I pulled my nose toward the ground to gain
airspeed. When my ailerons started to buzz I rolled
right and headed straight up, throttle still full. I was
now above and behind the remaining two Gothas. I
began a pass from the rear, diving at the port side of
the closest one. When I had the right lead I let the
Vickers speak, and I emptied the belt. I passed behind,
counting bullet holes and watching chunks separate
from the plane. A gunner fired at me but missed. Not
even close. I was up on the Gotha's right now. I cruised
out of range while I went through the Keystone Kops

procedure of changing bullet belts. Then I swung down for another pass. I tried for the engine. Perhaps I hit it, but I also shot away some struts. The right wings started a slow collapse, and that airplane was dying, also. I used the speed I had gained by diving on the second airplane to regain a perch. I pulled ahead of the last Gotha. I wagged my wings and waved before I turned away. I wanted him to live to tell the tale of the Purple Scourge.

I found some populated German trenches and used my remaining ammunition on strafing runs in the hope the troops would note the Purple Terror. Then it was time to go home.

***

For several months I enjoyed the hospitality of Mons. Poindex and daily forays into the sky in search of trouble. My first tangles with fighter were with Fokker D11's, which were essentially bi-plane Eindeckers. My modified Nieuport so easily outperformed them that it wasn't even sporting. I ran across Albatross D III's, with those V struts that weakened the wings and made them, too, easy prey. I was almost ashamed of myself. The German's were providing a carnival shooting gallery for me and the Vickers gun never once refused to shoot for me. At one point a German pilot, sighting the Purple Scourge, headed home before even getting close enough to engage. I could have chased him down, but some warning signal ran across my skin. It might be a trap. I let him go.

And, the following day, the warning signal was with me from takeoff. I don't believe in prescience, or anything supernatural for that matter. Yet I felt something significant was coming my way that day. I have always been disturbed when flimsy hypotheses, like that of God, seem to be proven by the occurrence of an event of very low but still finite probability. "My prayers were answered" is proof of nothing if the data doesn't include all the times the prayers *weren't* answered. A mother always has fears about the safety of her son. When he finally kills himself in an illegal drag race she gets to say, "I just knew something bad was going to happen tonight." Everyone else then gets to say, "Mothers know." But, as much as I hate to admit it, I knew something momentous was going to happen that day. It did.

I had flown north to the region around Somme. Trenches had been established, along with German air superiority. My job had come down to this; make the area safer for our reconnaissance flights by shooting down the German aces who were making the area dangerous for our reconnaissance flights. I was becoming the bad ass the Germans had to pay attention to, while our brave guys scouted the positions of German units and artillery and tanks and whatever else war on the ground entailed. The Good Guys Bad Ass against the Bad Guys Bad Assess. I loved that job. By then I was 85 and already questioning the value of living forever. To be honest, if I had known I would live another hundred years and see a smart phone in the pocket of a six year old child, I don't know if I would have been more or less reckless than I was.

At any rate, I got to the battlefield, and there they were: Fokker DR1's. Six of them. Just as I knew they were on my horizon before I saw that horizon, I knew that either von Richthofen or Voss or maybe both were in that squadron. I just knew it. And I knew that this time I couldn't run.

It was obvious they were looking for me, because they all broke in my direction at once, like a flock of starlings that makes an ever changing display in the sky. That had to the excitement of the hunt and not briefed tactics, for surely the leader of that pack would want the kill undisputedly his. This loss of discipline went to my advantage, perhaps my real salvation. It was another example of the luck which has followed me through life. If they had followed the leader I couldn't have beaten all of them. But they didn't follow the leader. They all went for the kill, and in the ensuing grab-ass my only problem was avoiding collision with one of the overeager pilots in that gaggle of Fokkers. The strength of the tri-plane was that it could turn inside almost any other aircraft, and it was very responsive to the Gnome engine. Now, as the air battle began, they were turning inside themselves, firing hesitantly for fear of hitting each other. I zigged and zagged, slowed and accerated, climbed and dove, rolled and looped. My own super-modified Gnome answered my every call, and in all my years, all my battles, all my adventures, I can't think of a greater sustained rush. I was breathing hard, and every now and then a Fokker would enter my field of vision, approaching on a line to cross my nose. I would fire a short burst. I know I hit some of them. I'll never know if I shot anyone down in that battle. It didn't matter. They had somehow gotten themselves into the worst possible tactic to down a single adversary. When I understood this, my head exploded with thoughts that would now seem impertinent to the fight, but which I couldn't help. I was flying pretty much by instinct anyway, since there was no sense in thinking too far ahead; I was besieged by random particles in a small box with no ordering laws.

One of my first musings concerned my philosophy concerning the efficacy of committees. I have always found that in a debate between an individual and a committee, the individual will always win. Why? Because the overall competency of any committee is always less than that of its least competent member. Put another way – as you add people to a thought process, the probability of bad ideas increases, ultimately masking the lone good idea.

This led me to think about the squadron leader, probably Voss or von Richthofen. He was almost certainly sitting in his cockpit screaming. If there had been radios at the time, he would have been screaming into one, painting the ears all his wingmen red. "Back off you fools! *Gott Sie dammt.*". But there were no airborne radios and hand signals would have been fruitless. You need a man steady beside you if you are to give a comprehensible hand signal. No. The leader was red in the face, the veins in his neck bulging, as he did exactly what I was doing – trying to keep from being killed by a lucky (or unlucky) Fokker.

Then I thought of the people on the ground below, watching eight seven airplanes, as one of them, a rather pretty shade of purple, stitched in and out of the flock. "What are those fools doing," they might be asking. Or, conversely, "Look at the consummate skills of those pilots as they chase the enemy." Or, "More stupid airplanes. I wonder if Hilda is fucking the postman while I sit in this damn trench." I could think of many possibilities, the least probable of which was, "That guy in the purple plane sure is lucky." The last, of course, was the correct observation.

But even my luck has its occasional burps. Or maybe I sometimes count on it too much. Let's just say that by not thinking ahead I put my own ass in a crack. As I swerved in and out of the Germans, taking occasional bursts and giving them in return, I didn't think about my faithful Vickers. It had never let me down, and I had perfected the practice of reloading the belts in flight. I had always assumed that my skill and the outstanding performance of my machine would allow me to do that at will. I was still thinking that when I noticed the enemy airplanes drifting away from me. One by one they made our cloud of busy aircraft expand, until they were all out of range. There came a moment in that grand ballroom when all the dancers, including any partner I might have had, had left the floor, and I was left open-mouthed, dancing to my own music. Then I noticed – my partner had detached himself from the crowd, and seemed to be beckoning me. This was going to be a waltz for two. Was it Immelmann? Voss? von Richthofen?

Of course I answered that thrown gauntlet. I turned toward the tri-plane and we immediately engaged. I knew the Fokker could turn with me; he probably thought my Nieuport was standard and he could turn inside me. I knew he had a good engine; he probably thought it was it was the equal of mine, pulling a more nimble airframe. And I know he was certain he was a better fighter pilot than I. So, that part of my luck held: I had been underestimated once again.

We swooped by each other and we both turned hard, looking for each other's tail, like two dogs sniffing each other's assess. Only we didn't need to sniff – we weren't going to be friends. He got his first surprise – as hard as he turned he couldn't cut me off. Of course, I had the very same experience. We circled each other, both planning a new tactic, both waiting to see what the other was planning. I was aware of the other German planes holding their distance, watching. Somehow their leader had waved them off. This was between the two of us. His wingmen had finally understood that. I needed to break the circle before my opponent did.

We were both in left banks. I rolled hard to the right, as hard was the Nieuport's wings could take. Perhaps he had been planning the same tactic. He was momentarily out of my vision. I had to gamble everything. I rolled inverted, went to full throttle, and pulled the nose through the horizon. My airspeed was greater than it should be, but Leplombe's beefed up wings held. The rpm was too great also, so I backed off the throttle while I searched for the tri-plane. There he was! Off to my right, wings level. As my nose was coming back through the horizon I pushed the throttle to the firewall once again. As I went through vertical going up he was directly over my head. I had an advantage now. If he turned away I would stop the climb with a rudder and roll onto his tail. If he came toward me I could continue the loop and roll out on top and behind him. He did neither, apparently waiting for me to make one gyration too many and give the advantage to him.

I stopped the climb with my rudder and rolled toward him. I wasn't on his tail, but I had him broadside. I had surprised a man who was used to less reckless and maybe less skilled pilots. I would have this chance for just a second or two. I pushed the left rudder to swing the nose to a lead position and pulled the trigger on the Vickers. It barked two or three times and went silent. My Vickers. My sweet reliable Vickers. How could it? Then I realized – it wasn't jammed. The belt was empty.

I had wasted all those shots on the wingmen. Now I was in no position to play the reloading waltz with the stick between my legs and time to fritter away. I had had my chance. Now I was slipping from hunter to prey. Was the whole thing a tactic by whoever was leading that flight of tri-planes, a scheme to get me to empty my gun while he waited to claim the kill? I felt stupid; at the very least unthinking. But I wasn't dead yet.

I goosed the Gnome engine to its max, and threw the belts of ammunition and anything else that was loose over the side. I needed to be as light as possible. I started a climb, aimed to pass behind the leader and well away from the buzz of other fighters. He could turn hard to get behind me, but that would kill off airspeed, airspeed he would need to trade for altitude. I should be able to get away as long as I climbed straight ahead at full power. That meant heading east into German territory. I could live with that. I had a place in mind, and I would keep the farm in Saint Chalon out of the war in the bargain. I might be back someday.

He did turn hard, so he did sacrifice airspeed. He came out on my tail, but too low and too far back to shoot at me effectively. I thought for a few moments I had lost him, but my mirror showed him trailing me, actually keeping up. He was going to follow me until I ran out of petrol. He probably had more flying time left, since he hadn't had to fly far to get the front, and we were ever deeper into his territory. He didn't have to come up and get me. He had only to keep me in sight and wait me out. It dawned on me that I was too hasty when I lightered my load. If I had some ammunition for the Vickers I was now free to load it. No. I couldn't second guess myself. The plan at the moment of crisis was to lose the enemy. I never expected to reengage von Richthofen that day. Still, I couldn't help but feel just a bit dumb.

I needed another plan now, and my first thought was the farm of On Ree and Louie. If I were going to be forced to land, it should be near a friendly spot in an otherwise unfriendly territory. I hoped I could make it as far as Chalet Violet. What better place for the Purple Nieuport to become a relic – beside that old relic purple castle.

We remained in this awkward dance for however long it took for Chalet Violet to come into sight. Oh, he may have slipped back a bit, but not nearly as much as I would have liked. Because I was racing instead of cruising, I was going through my fuel quite rapidly. I would have to act soon, while I still had control. A sputtering engine would be a death knell and I wasn't about to give in to the hound behind me after I had come this far. I wanted to write the ending to this particular battle myself.

As I passed the castle, well past the dairy farm, I acted. I pulled the throttle to idle, tugged the stick and jammed the left rudder pedal. The Nieport snap rolled and then went into a spin. I spun through my adversary's altitude before he could react and close. I knew he would chase me down, but he had to circle to do it, and it's hard to turn tighter than an airplane in a spin. He would have to retreat out and down to try to intercept me. I was pretty sure he wouldn't have time to do that. My problem now was to stay in the spin until the last second, recover, and land, all in one motion. I was just guessing at his reaction to a grounded airplane, but I was pretty sure he wouldn't want to damage it. The Nieuport had performed like no other Nieuport he had seen and it would be a valuable item to capture intact. I was also fairly certain that an unspoken code of honor would keep him from shooting at me once I was on the ground. The knights of the sky didn't try to kill each other like infantry men. I had betrayed my luck by being careless with the Vickers' ammunition. I hoped my luck wouldn't betray me back. It almost never did, especially if I had the probabilities on my side.

I amazed even myself at my landing. I let the airplane spin until I could almost count the blades of grass in the pasture. Then I popped the stick forward, stomped the opposite rudder, listened to the wind pick up in the struts, and came out wings level at stall speed just a few feet off the ground. I rolled to a stop, cut the engine just before it was going to die anyway, and stood beside my sweetheart, watching whoever it was circle for a landing.

It turned out to be von Richthofen. I was kind of hoping for that, since he was the most notorious. As I watched, he circled to land and then rolled to a stop right beside the Nieuport, almost as if we were squadron mates. I knew he was as good as his reputation. He stepped unhurriedly from the cockpit. "Hello," he said, in rather good English. "I'm Manfred Von Richthofen. And you, whose name I do not yet know, are my prisoner."

"You can call me Max," I said. "What you can't call me is your prisoner."

"I have forced you down in my territory." He stopped for a second. "Max? Truly?"

"No. But good enough. And you didn't force me down. I landed of my own volition. I won't be staying long."

"You landed because you were out of fuel and you flew the wrong way. Why I don't yet know."

"I'm sure you can reason that out."

His eyes showed understanding. "Ah. You are not from the airfields we know about, and you did not want to lead me there."

"That, and I was pointed this way when I tried to make my escape."

"I understand. That, however, is of no matter. You are now officially captured."

I made a small laugh. "How do you plan to complete this capture? Will you and I walk together to some prison?"

"No. You will wait here with your airplane while I fly to the nearest garrison. They will send men to pick you up and secure this interesting machine."

"None of that will happen. After you get back into your own machine and leave I will destroy my aircraft. With heavy heart, I might add. Then I'll be gone. You won't see me again. At least not on the ground."

"Do you really think you can make your way back to your own lines unaided."

"I'm certain of it."

He patted the gun at his side. "Not if I prevent you physically."

I guess he hadn't noticed my Webley. I didn't pat it. I drew it and leveled it at him. "You can't do that. What you can do is get back into your own plane and go. Wherever you want."

"That's quite ungentlemanly of you. I have defeated you in battle, you are in my territory, a warrior in enemy control. You can't shoot me now. We're not in the trenches, not at the front. Your battle is over. Honorably. You must maintain that honor."

"I don't see it that way. In the first place, I had you in my sights. I could have downed you."

"But you didn't, did you? Instead you foolishly used all your ammunition shooting at passing ghosts. Do you think I didn't expect that?"

I shrugged. "Did you also expect me to get into a position where you were dead in my gunsight? I should have won that joust."

He repeated, "But you didn't, did you?"

It really was my mistake, but I couldn't let that silent admission show. With a thin smile I said, "I will next time."

His smile was equally thin. "I see I made a mistake also. I should have had my own weapon drawn when I approached. But, you see, I expected you to be more of a gentleman." He cocked his head a little, as if reaching a decision. "I believe you really would shoot me if I made for my gun."

"Of course I would."

"Well, if you handle a pistol as well as you handle an airplane, I'd then be dead. That's the least desirable outcome. At least for me."

"For me, too. I'm enough of a gentleman to let you just fly away and continue the game. If I kill you, I want it to be in an airplane."

He was already climbing back into his cockpit. "I will try to send troops here to find you and appropriate your aircraft you know."

"Do what you want. I won't be here." I helped him kick over his engine.

***

He wasn't even airborne before I began to dismantle what I could of my dauntless craft. It hurt as I looked at her. She wasn't a horse with a broken leg. She was still sturdy and strong and willing, but I couldn't let her fall into enemy hands unless I deconstructed her and attempted to hide Leplombe's modifications which made her superior. I knew I didn't have much time. Von Richthofen would find the nearest post and send people to fetch her. I couldn't hold off a platoon of Germans while I did my work. It had to be now. I had to shoot a perfectly good horse.

I concentrated on the supercharger mechanism, which was of Leplombe's own design, and on the reduction gears, also innovative and important to the stunning performance. The Vickers gun had been good for me, but it was a standard Vickers and too heavy to run away with. It would stay as is.

There was a basic took kit stowed at about the center of gravity of the airplane, with just enough equipment to allow me access and removal of the parts I sought to seclude. I was glad it was out of reach of the cockpit, for I probably would have thrown it overboard when I was lightening load. I removed the parts I thought important, took one last look at that purple beauty, and blinked back a tear. A flare was the one last tool I needed. The fuselage would burn, and there would be just the right fume/air mixture in the fuel tank to make an explosion and some frame destroying heat. I did what I hoped I would never have to do again – kill a friend for the greater good. I set the fire just aft of the cockpit and took off running, secret parts in all my pockets and both hands. I could see Chateau Violet in the distance and made for it. I wasn't a hundred meters before I heard the explosion. I didn't look back, but ran another kilometer before I started scattering little screws and gears and rods, kicking dirt over them when I could, keeping a few for another kilometer, always heading toward the Chateau. From there I could find the farm blindfolded.

It was in fact dark when I knocked on the door and Henry answered.

Denis De Luchi

Chapter Eight

Night Work

There is this feeling in your gut

When you're doing something wrong

And you know it

There are no colors there at night

It is all in black and white

That's why you know it

You should go talk to her

There's a human love involved

You have to know it

There are guys who count on you

They're there and you are too

You can't not know it

But you do just what you do

It's all about just you

You prick. You know you know it.

These were the thoughts in Isaac Newton's head as he sat under an apple tree in Lincolnshire. The gravity thing occurred to him days later, when he spilled his soup in his lap.

Tall, thin Henry almost cried when he saw me standing at his door. "Louis, Louis." He tried to call out, but it was in trembling voice. Finally he had command of his vocal chords. "Louie! It's Alain," he yelled as he threw himself on me. I grunted at his strong hug and thought I felt tears on my neck. I have never felt so welcome. I almost didn't mind the smell.

Louis came running to the door. He pushed Henry aside. Being much shorter than Henry, I imagined Louis' tears on the front of my shirt. There were probably no tears anywhere, but the hugs were powerful. They exclaimed together, "You're back! Where did you come from? How did you get here?"

I described the day's activities as if giving a military debriefing. When I came to the part when I had to put the purple Nieuport out of its misery, that airplane we had so lovingly cared for, there really were tears. I said, "I know. I had to do it, and I know how much you treasured that machine. It was a good tool, a good servant, and many of the enemy will be haunted by its ghost." I suddenly felt the need for an imperative action. "First, before we open wine, I must know – do you still have contact with Sir David Carlyle?"

Henry frowned. "We are still in the war, but we talk now with something called MI6. It is new and they decide what is best for people like us to do. We are now connected by this secret radio. It is amazing. They handle all the communications and make the decisions, but I believe they can link us to Sir David. What is it you wish?"

"I need to get back into action. I had Von Richthofen in my sights once. Maybe I can do it again. At the very least, if I had a plane, I could terrorize some Germans. Or, still lesser than least, maybe this MI6 could give me something to do while I wait for a plane. Like help you fellows or something."

"Oh," said Louis, "that would be joyous. We blow things up, you know. Just like you did, only we sneak up on them, instead of flying to them. We don't get as many as you did. A train every now and then. A troop truck."

"But it all counts," added Henry.

"Yes." I had to agree. The more death and destruction one could perpetrate, the better. That was what war was all about. "But tell me, how do you know what and where? Does it all come over the radio from MI6?"

"Oh, yes," Henry said, casually. "This MI6 thing is very organized. We get messages in and out from that blurry-eyed miller down the road. I don't think you've ever met him. Fat old bastard. Dirty. Flour has worms. But he's true to the cause and he knows how to send messages and receive them. And no one would suspect. He seems stupid and nothing could come in and out of that old mill except grain and wormy flour.

Why? Do you want to send a message? To MI6? Would they even know who you are?"

"I want you to send a message for me. If it comes from you, they'll know who you're talking about. Is there some sort of code or something/"

The miller, Alfonse, knows about all that stuff. We have to trust him to get it right. He's the only guy who does. We used to call him Fat One, but we treat him with more respect now. Although we still call him Fat One."

"Good. Let me compose a message. But first, I'm hungry and thirsty."

"We can take care of that." Henry put his arm around my shoulder. "There is plenty of stew in the pot, and we just stole a few bottles of wine from the wine cave of a collaborator. That's our steady source of drink these days. He deserves to serve Belgians at least that much."

The stew was Louis' special ratatouille, the stuff I had gagged down before. I was so hungry I had a second helping. We drank a bottle of wine each.

Then it was time to compose a message. Here is what I asked Henry to send the next day through Fat Alfonse the miller and radio man extraordinaire.

For Sir David Carlyle-

Nieuport destroyed to keep from German hands. Details later. Need new airplane. Need ground mission until delivery. Purple Duke.

Then we were all sleepy. There was a back room they never used. The smell wasn't quite so bad there, so I got right to sleep. It's obvious that how deeply one sleeps is in direct proportion to how fatigued one is when he lies down. I slept like a sloth who had just won a race with a jaguar.

***

After a deplorable but probably nutritious breakfast, Henry headed down the road to the mill. We had decided I should stay out of sight, although I could remain in the farmhouse. Henry, as did almost everyone in the district, had reason to go to the mill. Only a trusted few knew that the miller was a radio man. By a few I mean On Ree, Louie, and a very old geezer who might have served under Napoleon. He hated Germans and did what he could to discomfort them. It wasn't much. Pissing in their wine barrels – that sort of thing. In fact he was an old friend of Fat One and his resistance comrades had started calling him The Pisser. So I had on my side On Ree, Louie, Fat One, and The Pisser. I could hardly wait to see what my mission with them would be.

But all Henry returned with was the assurance my message had been received and that the return transmission told me to wait a day while MI6 worked something out.

***

The nest day was Louis' turn to run down to the mill. He was gone a long time, long enough to cause concern to Henry. I wasn't worried. I suspected MI6 wanted to verify operations with Sir David, and also work out a suitable ground mission for me. I didn't expect the Nieuport to be replaced instantly.

I was right. When Louis returned he had all sorts of news. First, Sir David was glad I had destroyed the first purple Nieuport, and Leplombe was already building an even better one. Next, thanks to me, Henry and Louis had been given their first really big mission. There was a German ammo dump just south of the town of Dinant. It was to be destroyed. Set off. Blown up. MI6 thought I was just the man to lead the sabotage effort. If I had been in England I would have pointed out that I could fly airplanes well, shoot guns well, and kill people with my bare hands well, but I really knew very little about making explosives work, other than throwing hand grenades out of airplanes. It would have been a good argument there. Here in the little dairy farm west of Bastogne, transmitting in short bursts over a radio, it would carry no weight. Besides, I had nothing better to do for a while, and On Ree and Louie were like schoolboys over the prospect. A day or two to travel north, some sneaking around, and then a series of big explosions. They would truly be in the war then.

Still, I had to be honest with them. "I know it sounds like a good thing to do, but I'm no explosives guy. If we're going to make the munitions dump go off, we need to know what we're doing. Do either of you know how to make explosives explode?"

They both shook their heads. Then Henry brightened. "But I know someone who does."

"Really? And he's one of us?"

"Sure. You know him too. It old Bartel. The Pisser."

"He can barely move about. Even if he could make the trip, how do I know he knows anything about setting off munitions?"

"He was in the navy. Firing big guns was his job."

"Is that the world renowned, much feared Belgian Navy?'

"Don't make fun. We have ships with big guns. You have to know how to use them safely, and how to set off the charges. I daresay, he's an expert."

"I guess I have no choice. How do we get him there?"

"We travel by horse cart. One man driving, everyone else hiding in the hay."

I looked over at Louie. "Tell me, Louis, do you think that is a good idea? Do you think the Germans won't jump all over a one way hay cart? Plodding along from here to Dinant, as if they have no hay there?"

Louie shook his head. "Surely someone, somewhere, will poke the hay," he said.

"Exactly," I said. "So we travel on foot, at night, and hide in the daytime. We travel light and fast. The Pisser can't walk that far."

"So what's your solution?" On Ree asked.

"I learn from The Pisser. He teaches me what I need to know. It should take just a few hours, if that."

"And then we go." They said it together. They were that eager.

***

It would have been that simple, except while I was being tutored by The Pisser in how to make things that go bang go bang when you want them to, On Ree made one last trip to the Fat One's radio shack. When he came back, he had interesting news. "There is another problem for you to solve," he said. To my shrug and expectant look, he continued. "You are not to come back here after Dinant. You are to proceed back to

Saint Chalon. By the time you get there you will have your new airplane."

That was exciting. Still, there was that extra problem. "Won't I have to cross through German territory, German lines, perhaps the battlefields? How do they expect me to do that. I am a good navigator, especially in an airplane, but I don't know the countryside. And the countryside doesn't know me. If the Germans don't shoot me, the French or the English will. I need to bypass a lot of people and places to show up at Saint Chalon."

"MI6 must have thought you would say that. Their last words were, 'know you can do it.'"

Maybe I could, but at that moment I wasn't seeing how. I was ready to slip into a thought funk when The Pisser spoke. That dear old wizened man. He had given me rudimentary knowledge about making explosions without killing myself, and he had one more gift. "You need a guide," he said.

"No, Pisser, we've already said you can't come. And then all the way through battle lines to Saint Chalon? No."

"Not me," he said.

"Who? You know somebody we can trust, besides Henry and Louis?"

Yes."

"Who?"

"My granddaughter."

I looked at On Ree. He held his hands out, palms up, in that 'don't ask me' gesture. Louie was a little more involved. "Pisser," he said, "you've always said you wanted to keep her out of this business."

"That is true. But this is a chance for her to get out of here. To get to a safe place in France until this stupidity is over. The Germans will start to notice her, even though I keep her hidden from them. But she's a woman now, and I feel her being less safe every day."

"But....a guide?"

The Pisser gave a reassuring wave. "Before this war she traveled with her father quite a bit. She knows Southern Belgium and Central France well. She's strong and she's smart. Let her be your guide and do both of us a favor." When The Pisser said this he looked less like a doddering old man and more like a thoughtful parent. Or grandparent, as the case might be.

I considered. "Three things," I said. "One, swear she is trustworthy. Two, does she really know how to safely navigate through the lines? And, three, can she keep up?"

The Pisser smiled. "One, I would trust her with my life. And therefore, yours. Three, she's as strong as you. So, there is Two. And you won't know that until you try. Until she sees what and who is where. I guarantee you won't make it without her. Your chances are better than even with her."

Since I have always believed that life is at it basis a series of probabilities, and better than even is a good bet, especially if it is the only bet, I didn't hesitate. "Get her ready. We leave tomorrow."

Chapter Nine

One Step at a Time

You got to know just one thing

You got to travel light

Cause given all the detours

It's hard to get it right

Sure evil's in the forest

Lurking in the trees

But if you travel light enough

You're by it like a breeze

Sure every woman's lovely

You'd love to dally there

But if you take her with you

She'll double up your fare

So get on down the road man

Leave loves and friends behind

There'll be new ones comin' later

More than you wish to find

Clean socks and greenback dollars

Are all you need to bring

And when the journey's over

Lift your head and sing

Hum gazza gazza gazza

Hum gazza gazza gazza

What gazza what gazza

Have I gazza done

The great jazz trumpeter Bieder Bixbeck wrote this for
his eighth wife, Louisiana Lulu. She was also his twelfth
wife, but what he wrote her then is said to be
unprintable.

See. That's the thing about this immortality business. You're always saying goodbye, and the people you're saying it to don't understand that you really mean it. With most people it doesn't matter all that much. You kind of liked them or you kind of disliked them or maybe you're happy you'll never see them again, But there are people you really care about, you love, you've shared those life altering moments with. People you give a shit about and it hurts twice. One, you feel guilty because they don't know that as far as you're concerned, they're dead. And two, you really love them and it rips at your guts. You try and you try. You live a hundred years, two hundred years, and you vow never to let another person into your gut, your heart, your head. And you keep fucking up and letting them in.

This time was especially tough. On Ree and Louie were like brothers, mates. I had flown off, leaving them with tears in their eyes, promising we'd meet again, knowing that I was lying. Although as it turned out, I wasn't lying, no thanks to me. So this was like having a funeral for your best friend, putting him in the ground, and then having him resurrected, smiling, only to have to put him back into the ground. Henry and Louis tried to be stoic, but they both had that teary-eyed grimness usually saved for the ghost of one of Henry VIII's wives. Reincarnated, they were becoming ghosts again. I vowed I would never come back to their dairy farm outside Bastogne. I acknowledged even then I had a bad record vice vow-keeping.

Then there was The Pisser. He was sending his granddaughter on a dangerous journey in the care of a feckless pilot. He was really in bad shape. He wanted to keep her close, to protect her. He also knew if he kept her close he couldn't protect her. He hated the Germans, and he wanted to fight them, but he was too old. He knew I could fight them for him, and fight them well. He wanted me to succeed. She could help me do that. He had to trust me with her, to be her shield and not her downfall. He wasn't sure he could do that. He had no choice. He was crying. Crying and trembling. He grabbed me. "I will always honor you if you get her safely to France. I will pray to whatever god you wish to deliver you both. I put her in your hands, as you put yourself in hers. Don't fail me. Don't let harm come to her. Bring it to those who would do her harm. Go and......" He broke down, sobbing. In the coming weeks those tears would turn to urine in many German wine barrels.

I don't know if Fat One cared if I stayed or went. I never met the man, although I did eat biscuits made with his wormy flour. He was obviously a damn good radio man.

***

I had finally torn Joan away from her grandfather,

and myself away from On Ree and Louie. We were in the hay cart, heading north, she driving, dressed as a man, me ensconced in the hay with the few things I need to wreak mayhem on the German munitions dump at Dinant, plus some food and wine. She had cut her hair short and wore a peasant cap. She had an ill-fitting rough wool suit and ankle high boots. I guess she looked enough like a skinny farm boy to give us the courage to try this daytime travel. I was dubious. In that cart, fully clothed and covered with hay, I felt naked. When a German troop truck almost ran us off the road I'd had enough. We weren't being courageous. We were being stupid. As I've said before, there may be no difference. I asked her to pull the cart behind the next stand of trees. We needed to return to my original suggestion – travel by night, on foot.

When we were safely out of sight of the road, she climbed down and I climbed out. "What's the matter?" she asked. She was calm and her voice was steady.

I had accepted her as a guide from the first moment I saw her. At our first meeting she had worn a tight fitting short sleeved shirt and long pants. I assumed she did this to show me she was fit and muscular. Her hands showed she had done the work of a farm youth. Her demeanor was one of confidence, and her face and voice indicated awareness but little fear. When she looked at me, first in the eyes and then up and down, I knew I was being appraised as well. I passed muster.

She was pretty enough for any venue, a little shorter than I, her short hair an attractive shade of brown. Her eyes were deeper brown. Here, behind the trees, she stood with hands on hips, ready to argue. Her femininity had been disguised by some smudges on her face and the postures she had taken pains to learn. "Well, what's the matter," she repeated.

"The matter is," I said, "that we can't expect to go all the way to Dinant like this. Some truck, some car will not merely force us to the side, it will stop. At a passing glance, you look like a young male driving a hay cart. The key word is 'passing.' Someone is going to stop and look at you closely. Then they will poke in the hay with a rifle barrel. In there, I am in no position to put up a fight. I'd be lucky not to get a gun barrel up my ass."

"So, you waited until now to avoid arguments with my grandfather and the others."

"I waited until now to see if I could stand it. I can't."

"But there's so much to carry."

"That's what we have rucksacks for. You take some stuff. I can carry most of it."

"You think you're that tough?"

"I have to be. We won't get there in a hay cart in the daylight. And who drives a hay cart at night?"

She only took a moment to decide I was right. "Let's say you can do it. We still have to deal with the horse."

I liked that. She wasn't intimidated by the danger inherent in the trip. She thought in the moment, and that meant caring about the horse. "There's plenty of food in this field. He can't eat it faster than it grows. He's a horse. He's as tough as we are. Tougher."

"So. Do you want to stay here until night?"

"We could. Or we could see how well we travel on foot, for just a little bit. Maybe find a safer bivouac. I notice some farm houses on the western horizon. If we stay east of the road we should be safe for a while. You ready to walk?"

"Yes. Let's get on with it."

We walked until early afternoon. She easily kept up with my brisk pace, but I felt it was nearing time to rest if we were going to travel further that night. I started searching for a spot to stretch out and nap. While I was so engaged, I felt a tap on my shoulder. When she had my attention, she nodded at a dot on the horizon. I recognized it as the first farmhouse we had seen in sometime. "We might be able to stop there," she said.

"I don't think so. I don't want any more contact with people than necessary."

"We could at least look it over."

"Fine." I didn't see any purpose in that, since my mind was made up, but we were still a long way from the house. I felt the issue would resolve itself without argument. She was my guide, but I was the boss. Looking couldn't hurt, as long as no one was looking back.

About half a kilometer from the house she tapped my shoulder again. We were at the property's fence line and I was ready to circumnavigate the place, but she pointed to a mark at the base of a fence post. "What's that?" It looked like a child had been playing with paint.

"It the Belgian tricolors," she said. "It's a sign the householder is a patriot. We would be safe there."

"You're sure?"

"See if there isn't such a mark on nearly every post between here and the house." Sure enough, as we advanced past four such posts, three of them had the black, yellow, and red stripes inauspiciously painted at the bottom. I was still against going to the house and said so. "I understand your caution," she said. "But I would like some intelligence on what might be ahead." I had to admit that made sense.

We approached the house as innocent hikers would, without looking over our shoulders, walking casually. In case anyone inside were watching, we needed to look like what we pretended to be. Joan did this well, with just a few words of instruction from me. She knocked. I was going to let her do the talking. She had the regional accent. The opening door showed a squinty-eyed older fellow, leathery faced, with a few days gray stubble. He didn't speak; just stared at us expectantly. This discomfited Joan, but it was up to her to start the conversation.

Her composure kicked in. "We're sorry to disturb you, but we're traveling by foot through your countryside, and we want to be sure we're headed in the right direction. Perhaps you can help us. We want nothing more than a little information and perhaps a drink of water."

He squinted even more severely, fixing especially on my rucksack. The tension in the shoulder straps revealed its weight. "You may be on foot, but you're not traveling light." He was no fool. I hoped he was on our side. I felt an urge to speak, to feel him out, but I had to trust Joan to do that.

"We're carrying all we could take with us. Our village is no longer habitable, if you understand my meaning."

The old man's eyes under that squint were gray, essentially colorless, and gave nothing away. He looked at Joan expressionlessly. "You're a girl. Why are you dressed like a man?"

She didn't miss a beat. "We thought it would be safer for me. You know. The Boche."

"Yes," he said. "The Boche." They both surprised me, using the French pejorative for Germans. I hadn't heard it used by Belgians before this. The man looked again at my rucksack. "So, what are you carrying?"

I had to let Joan carry the conversation, since my Belgian French sounded like English French. I hoped she would come up with something plausible. "Hard cheese, a couple of bottles of wine, a couple of things precious to us." That sounded reasonable to me.

It didn't to him. "Looks heavy enough to be gold," he said.

"I wish it were," Joan said. "That would make the trip easier. We could bribe our way along. But nobody wants moldy cheese or my father's poor wine. I do have a gold cross in my own pack, but it's small, and I'd never give it up anyway. It was my mother's." She crossed herself, kissed her fingers, and reached back to pat her own backpack. It was done with such sincerity and grace I almost believed the fusing mechanisms in that pack were her sainted mother's precious crucifix.

Old squinty gray-eyes was unimpressed, but he said, "I suppose I can spare some food and wine. Put your packs there in the corner. Perhaps you might even want to spend the night. You could sleep on the hay in the barn." When Joan looked querulously at me, his squint turned to frown of suspicion. "I presume you two are married. Why doesn't your husband speak?" So, he had noticed. His next question was directed specifically to me. "We should introduce ourselves," he said. "My name is Lauran Tartaq. No 'e'. And you are...?"

I cleared my throat. "Jean. Jean Montpelier." I tried for the accent. I couldn't read his face to tell if I succeeded.

"And I am Joan Montpelier," Joan added, to assure him we were married.

He grunted. "Well, if I'm going to help you, we might as well start with dinner. I have some bread and leftover roast. Cold. Some cheese from a neighbor. It's not bad. Some wine, also from a neighbor. It's not that good, but he tries, and I have to accept the gift. I can't throw it away." He saw me glance at the fireplace, which had no fire. "I only cook for myself every few days. And it's still warm out. No need for a fire." I thought it strange that he felt the need to justify his lifestyle choices. Besides, there was a little wood burning stove with its own chimney, not quite in a corner. Obviously the cottage was built around a fireplace, as most old cottages were. The wood stove came later. Why worry about me looking at a cold fireplace? I let that thought go as we sat down on rough chairs at the rough table to eat.

He was right. The cheese was not bad. The meat was dry and almost tasteless. The bread was stale and Tartaq was right about the wine, too. It was close to vinegar. Still, it all represented hospitality, if by a grudging host. Joan and I had put in a hard day without expecting any hospitality anyplace, so I admonished myself for being judgmental. And the fellow was going to give us bed and shelter in the bargain. All that gave him the right to run through the entire dinner with only a few grunts and wheezes by way of communication. The only complete sentences he uttered the entire time came when Joan tried to start a conversation about possible German strengths and locations. He said curtly, "I know nothing about what the Germans are up to. I try to stay out of their way." We weren't asking for a floor show a la Moulin Rouge – only a little information. Maybe, if I lived in this place, the way this man lived, I would be a grouch, too. Still, there were little red flags waving in my head.

The last bit of cheese had disappeared. Abruptly, and a propos of nothing, Tartaq said, "I want you two out of here now. Go, if you wish, and sleep in the barn. Don't come back in here tonight, and make yourselves gone before breakfast. If anyone should find you there, you snuck in there without my knowledge.

Understand?" When we nodded, he said, "Just stay in there and don't come out until you leave. At dawn. Understand?" We nodded again. Then he simply grunted. As I started toward the corner to retrieve out packs, he started to say something more but seemed to think better of it. During dinner, between grunts and wheezes, he had eyed those packs. He was obviously curious about them. Apparently he had decided he could do nothing about that curiosity. I wondered if I could do something about my own.

In his rude manner he saw us out the door and pointed toward the barn. Then he followed us there. It was almost too dark to navigate inside that place and he hadn't bothered to bring the lone lantern that had lighted our supper. He merely stood at the barn door and indicated a spot straight ahead. "Walk straight," he said. "There's horseshit to your left I haven't cleaned out yet. The hay pile is straight ahead." My accurate horseshit sensing device told me he wasn't lying. There was a lot of horseshit in that barn. Before we could reply, let alone act, he slammed the door closed and was gone. We didn't get to thank him for the gourmet meal.

Joan and I held and hands inched our way forward until we bumped into a hay pile. Since the odor of horse manure was so strong, we couldn't tell if the hay was piled on some of it. Joan asked, "Should we lie down in this stuff?"

"Let's hold off on that," I said. "I'm probably wrong, but there may be better places to rest."

"What do you mean?"

"Well, Tartaq is a weird old man, and weird old men get to act strangely. But this fellow triggers some alarms. I need to be sure he's merely what he seems to be, in which case we can rest in the hay and getting up smelling bad, or we can leave now and camp a ways down the road. But suppose he's not only a weird old man, but a bad one, too. Suppose he wants to give us up to the, as you say, Boche."

"But how could he do that? I would guess it's a long way to any Boche quarters. I don't think he could travel at night. And we'll be gone before he is in the morning."

"Two things. If he had to travel to inform on us, it would take time, that's true. But it would still make the Germans aware that we were about. With good descriptions, too. But there's another way to communicate. Fat One does it well."

"Radio." I could see she was angry with herself for not having thought of it. She didn't want to give in. "I still think he just an old farmer living by himself and it was hard for him to be hospitable. That doesn't make him a bad person."

"I hope you're right. But I wouldn't be having this worry if I hadn't let you talk me into coming here, so the problem is mine. I'll just feel better if I check on him. I'll try not to let him know about it."

"I suppose," she said, sitting in the hay, "I should be glad you're so careful. You're right, of course. We shouldn't take any unnecessary chances."

"Then I wish you had waited until I got back before you made yourself comfortable. You're going to be hard to travel with if you come out of this smelling like horseshit."

"I'm a farm girl. I've smelled like horseshit many times. It hasn't kept the boys away."

I grinned at this pretty young girl. "Farm boys are so used to horseshit they don't notice it. They could pick up on fertile female smells. And, of course, you're very attractive."

"I didn't think you had noticed."

"It's not a priority. Just stay put till I get back."

I headed carefully toward the barn door, trying to retrace our route in through the pitch black of the barn. I tried to picture the route, stepping carefully. Stepping in manure wouldn't have been fatal, but I really didn't want to sneak around Tartaq's house smelling like a horse with dysentery. When I finally reached the door

muck free, I tested it gingerly. It opened. He hadn't
tried to lock us in. I guessed he realized that we might
have to go out to relieve ourselves, and an attempt at
imprisonment would be a giveaway. You can see that I
was already prejudiced against him. Joan probably
knew that. I didn't care. For our safety I had to
presume everyone guilty until proven innocent.
Frankly, I didn't see any way to prove Tartaq's
innocence. In that situation, there were no benefits of
the doubt. Maybe if I found him passed out drunk I
might think him benign, but even then he would have to
sleep through my seven-kicks-to-the-head-and-body
test.

Outside there was a bit more light than in the barn.
The moon was not quite at first quarter. I could make
out the cottage, and even see a thin line of light where
the closed shutters of the glassless window didn't quite
meet. That meant he hadn't gone straight to bed; he
wouldn't be burning oil if he had. I doubted that he was
reading Voltaire. It took me a while to reach that
shuttered window. In the dark I had to test every
footstep, to be sure I didn't snap a twig or step on a
squealing critter. The crack that let out the light would
let in an anomalous sound from the otherwise quiet
night. The time it took to cover that thirty meters or so
tested my patience, rubbed my nerves raw, but
hardened my resolve to carry out the required
surveillance. I didn't doubt this precaution was
necessary, and I had come this far.

I was finally next to the window, which was really just a square hole in the cottage wall, closed to the outside by the bulky wooden shutters. I began to hear someone speaking, Crouching just below the thin space between the ill-fitting window doors, I tried to get an ear placed for maximum audibility. I didn't want to stick my head up. There might be enough light coming through the crack to make an outside object noticeable. I said 'shit' several times while my mental gears turned without catching. Then I remembered a map in my jacket's vest pocket.

The map rolled nicely into a tube, and with one end of that tube at the bottom of the crack and the other in an ear, the indistinct speech resolved. It was Tartaq. He was speaking in German.

I could understand enough to know he was communicating with some regional German command post, since the conversation was between him and some unintelligible static. Unintelligible, but German. He was a bad guy Fat One. My mental gears went whirling again, at first with considerations that were irrelevant to the immediate problem. Was Tartaq a paid traitor or just misanthropic? Why did I care? What was urgent here? It would be nice to know what he had told the Germans thus far. Wait. Did that matter? No. All that mattered was excape. But suppose he hadn't given our descriptions yet. Suppose the report had just started. It would be best to silence Tartaq before we left. Modern fans of horror movies should understand this. If you don't kill the monster he always gets up from behind the couch to make more trouble.

I reached down the back of my pants and found the handle of my Webley. I had almost sat on it through dinner, with its bulge covered by my jacket bottom. It had six rounds in it. I only needed one. I thought I might use more than one, to emphasize my profound distaste for betrayers. Now I needed to know how to get in. My gears had downshifted, providing less unproductive whirring and more torque to climb the solution mountain. I could picture the door from the inside. There was no great bolt. He didn't need one; his neighbors were friendly and he was in cahoots with the Germans. There was a simple rope lash to hold it closed.

So, there came about the sudden and unexpected death of Lauran Tartaq, when an angry but self-controlled man burst through his flimsy rope lash, caught him sitting by his fireplace with a wire up the chimney and a radio transmitter attached to the wire, and shot him. Directly between the astonished eyes, from a distance of about seven paces. And then shot him once more, in the heart, from even closer range. Just to keep the monster dead behind the couch.

I took the lantern with me when I returned to the barn. When I flung open the barn door and illuminated the inside, I could see that Tartaq really hadn't cleaned out the place in a while. Too busy betraying his countrymen, I suppose. But there was Joan, still sitting in the hay. She was a patient woman, especially given the circumstances. The time for such patience was over. Now it was time to act. "I hate to tell you this, but we must move on. Right now. And we have to put as much space between this place and us as possible. At dawn we'll find a place to hide and rest."

"Then Tartaq....."

"Was a traitor. He was on the radio with the Germans when I got to the house. I killed him."

"Just like that?"

"Just like that. But I don't know what he was able to tell them. And I don't know how long it will take them to get here. I expect they want to come while it is still dark, so that no one can see them capture us on Tartaq's place. That's why we must hurry."

"I suppose you had to kill him. Do we just leave his body lying around?"

"We don't have time to dig a grave. Besides, I'm not qualified to say a requiem mass. Are you?"

"It seems so barbaric to just leave him there."

"This isn't the first man I've killed. It's always barbaric. In war we have to become barbarians. We lose our humanity, bit by bit, one killing at a time. The only salvation is surviving the conflict, and doing good, bit by bit, to try to get the humanity back. Some people can do this. Don't ask about me."

I topped off Tartaq's kerosene lantern. I also grabbed the stale bread and the bit of dry roast that was left. I gave Joan a swig from the wine bottle, took one myself, and placed the bottle by Tartaq's body, along with a small crust of bread. "There's his mass," I said.

***

We strode through the night, lighting Tartaq's freshly oiled lantern when the moon went down. Joan was uncomplaining. Conversation was difficult, since we were in unfamiliar territory and it was so dark. At one point, with a hint of frustration in her voice, she said, "I'm supposed to be guiding you. I feel useless. You'd be better off without me."

"Nonsense," I said. "As long as we're going in generally the right direction, you'll recognize the country around Dinant when we see it in daylight. You'll get me there. And remember, we have second mission. To get you safely France. That will happen too. Just one thing. No more asking to spend the night in the manger." This seemed to pacify her.

As the sky started to lighten and I put out the lantern and began thinking about a bivouac, Joan voiced what was really troubling her. I was picking our way through some brush when she spoke to my back. "I thought about before we left. Having to kill someone I mean. I knew it was something we might have to do. I thought I could just accept it, just a necessity in certain situations. But it's not real until it happens. I didn't even see it happen. Just a grumpy old man who gave us dinner, and then he was a corpse. And we just left him there. Like discarded old clothes. I thought I was tough and hated the Boche. But he was a Belgian, and not a soldier. And he didn't have gun or even a sword. Why do I want to cry for him? Why aren't I tough like you?"

"It's not your job. Believe me, you don't want to be like me. On so many levels, you don't want to be like me."

She was quiet for a few steps. Then she said, "I suppose we'll have to kill again before we're through."

"Almost certainly. Maybe a guard around the munitions dump. Maybe someone who gets in our way." I heard her sigh, so I added, "Your grandfather wouldn't have me do less."

Denis De Luchi

Chapter Ten

The Big Bang

Give me your hand, my child

I'll guide you part of the way

You'll be on your own, my child

When you see my feet turn to clay

And when you decide, my child

Which way you want to ride

Don't curse my absence, child

Just keep in mind that I tried

From a note written by Phillip of Macedon when he told Alexander to get the fuck out of Macedonia.

The sun was just barely above the horizon when we found some brush thick enough to hide two weary travelers. The morning chill was still in the air, so when we lay down on the topsoil and leaves we had brushed together for a bed, we just naturally clung together for warmth. It didn't take long for either of us to enter sleep.

The sun was a little past zenith when I awoke. I found my arm stiff from being under Joan throughout our deep sleep. I tried to slide it free without disturbing her. I wasn't successful. She didn't awake with a start. She knew where she was and why. She said, "I needed that. I've never been so tired."

"We both did. Now we need a little sustenance." I broke out the dry roast and stale bread and a good bottle of wine. We had, given the circumstances, a feast. We now relaxed under our brush cover. I could see a few clouds through the leaves, so I lay back and let the cloud shapes play in my imagination. It was a pleasant diversion, and we had nothing else to do until sundown.

I thought Joan was doing the same thing until she said, "I'm almost ashamed of myself. No. I *am* ashamed of myself."

"I can't imagine why. You've escaped what could have been a nasty situation, and you've marched like a young infantryman. You've held up well; better than most men I think. You should be proud."

"But you see, that's the problem. I *am* proud. Even exhilarated. It seems wrong somehow."

"Proud and ashamed at the same time." I tried to hide my smile. "Welcome to the world of winner lives, loser dies. That's the world we're in right now. That's the world all those fellows in the trenches are in all the time. That's the world I'm in when I do combat in airplanes. I feel the thrill of victory when I shoot down an enemy. And I feel sadness when I kill a good pilot. Then I'm ashamed of myself for caring, and ashamed of myself for wanting not to care. Every possible emotion in generated in the aftermath of mortal combat. At least, in the normal person. You have to accept those feelings and still carry on. Still survive. That's what we're doing, and what we'll keep on doing until we cause an explosion in Dinant and escape to France. Don't let anything drive our mission from the top of your list of things to do today. And tomorrow and every day, until we are safe in France."

She didn't say anything for a long while, watching me watch the clouds. Then she leaned close and whispered in my ear, "There's more. More confusion. More shame."

I sat up and looked at her squarely. "What more?"

"This whole thing....you....killing Tartaq........running through the night......this rough picnic as if we were two teens on a Sunday outing......the thought of what lies ahead....it's all too stimulating.....even sexually."

I could no longer concentrate on elephants or big-titted women or flying reptiles in the clouds. She was presenting an unwanted distraction. "That's not unusual." I tried to be casual. "The first time escaping real danger can trigger all sorts of thoughts, even attraction to a comrade of the opposite sex. I'm sure it will pass." I couldn't tell her that if we were at a café on the Left Bank drinking absinthe I wouldn't let it pass. But then, it might not come up in the first place, since it was triggered by danger and death. "Just relax. Perhaps another little nap. Tonight will be another hard journey."

She wouldn't let it go. "And what? You have no feelings for me, no desire at all? Am I now that unattractive, with the grime and sweat of the hike? When I think of it, you've never once looked at me the way men look at women when they're thinking about possible romance. What's wrong?"

The whole thing wasn't hard enough, without having to become a half-ass Freud, but I didn't want even a marginal emotional attachment to yet another woman I would be forced to abandon. That doesn't mean I was being considerate of her feelings. In this situation it would be easy enough to let them think that all I cared about was the mission. No. It was selfish. I fell in love so damned easily it made every goodbye a bruising experience. In a hundred and eighty something years, my soul has been battered black and blue. I was finally learning that I needed to keep the bruises down to a minimum. "There's nothing wrong with you," I said. "There is a woman in England whom I love, to whom I made certain vows. Would you want me to break those vows just because you're a lovely woman who momentarily feels sexually stimulated?"

She had been ready to debate, but my reply gave her thought. I wasn't going to tell her that my relationship with Nancy was essentially over. Nancy just didn't know it yet. I needed to keep this arrangement with Joan strictly professional. It had to be that way, hard as it seemed. I was tired of finding ways to exit a woman's life that entailed mendacity and/or faux mortality. I wanted this to be, on a farm in France, a handshake. Good work and good luck.

Joan broke my chain of thought. "So, if I'm just to be a team member, what's my next assignment?"

That was a relief, and it brought me back to focus on the problems at hand. "Well, you can think about how we can get a little food. Thanks to the leftovers we lifted from Tartaq, we have about two days nourishment with us, provided we are careful and willing to stay a little hungry. I figure there are about five days, if we travel hard, before we are in a safe place in France. So, we need to get a little food, or be prepared to go hungry for a while. Any plan to acquire food needs to take risk versus benefit into account. Remember: it's better to go hungry than get caught. You're a farm girl. Think of ways we might find sustenance without finding the wrong end of a German bayonet. We have a difficult mission and some hard traveling to do. We should have the food energy to do that."

She nodded and lay back. She was thinking about it, which was a relief to me. Better that than romance.

***

I'll end my digression concerning food. We wound up stealing root vegetables. Anything but potatoes, since we couldn't make fires. I have lived, at times, high on the hog. Never much lower than living on stolen root vegetables, eaten cold.

***

It was the third night after our hasty departure from Tartaq's residence. We had scouted the German munitions depot in Dinant, and were waiting for the moon to set to carry out our sabotage. In those days there were no electric sensors in the ground around sensitive facilities. There were two guards outside the wire fence that circled the building. They walked around that perimeter, almost never in sight of one another. We could slither up to the fence after one of the perimeter guards had passed. We would have about seven minutes before the other came by, which gave us plenty of time for more slithering toward the building itself. There were no searchlights or guard towers, and inside the fence there were guards only at two ends of the building, at the only doors. They couldn't see each other, although they could call out to the passing sentries, which they didn't always do. Guards are guards. Some are better than others, but all slough off at one time or another. The guard at the end of the warehouse we had chosen called out about every other time a sentry passed. Sometimes he missed two passes. That meant that we could have about fourteen minutes to get in, set the charges, and get out before the fireworks lit the night. It was enough time if we worked quickly, efficiently, and allowed nothing to distract us. I had to impress that on Joan, who was up to the task but new to this kind of intrigue.

I took her by the shoulders, and forced to look directly into my eyes. "Once we start, once the clock has started ticking, you must not let anything distract you. I will have to kill the guard, and this time you will have to witness it. You can't dwell on that. After we enter, I will go along and set the charges. You will follow and set the fuses. You must not lose confidence in your ability. You know how to do it. Don't second guess yourself. Do what you know how to do and move quickly to the next charge. When we get to the end you will retrace our route and head for the exit. I will follow and activate the fuses. I want you not to hesitate, not to wait for me. I want you to be at least at the fence when I exit the building. Don't stop for anything, and don't worry about me. I will join you before the explosions. I'm not in the mood to be blown up tonight. Tell me you are determined to do exactly what I have said."

"I am," she said, with amazing nonchalance. So we settled to wait for the necessary darkness.

A first quarter moon sets around midnight. It seemed to take at least a hundred hours from sunset to midnight that night. Maybe longer. When the moon was gone and the sentry came by, we were more than ready, but there was no exchange between the door guard and the perimeter walker. "We'd better wait for the next sentry," I whispered. Joan made the slightest of nods. Again, there was no exchange. When I touched her shoulder she sighed, a little too loudly I thought. Finally, the third walker called out, "Nice night." "If you like this shit," was the reply. "You could be in the trenches if you want real shit." There was no reply. The threat of shit in the trenches was both figurative and literal.

When the sentry was safely past, we began our crawl to the fence. I could lift the snagging wire to let Joan through, and she held it up while I side the packs through and pulled myself, belly to dirt, inside the fence. We were just out of sight of guard, so we could run at a crouch to the corner of the building. I peeked around. The guard was inside the shallow portal, leaning against the jam. I could just see his shoulder. "Wait until I signal, then come fast." She nodded and I began to edge along the wall toward my target, knife in hand.

Okay, let's talk about skill and luck. I was taught Eastern martial arts and use of all sorts of weapons at an early age, and I have trained in both all my life. I am therefore adept in situations like the one I am describing. In addition, I have always been lucky, luck of the kind that one doesn't make himself, starting with the DNA quirk that prevents me from aging. Oh, I made a habit, early on, of calculating probabilities, but I found that even when the odds were much less than even I usually won the bet. I don't know why that is, any more than I understand the DNA business. That just the way it is.

So, when I carelessly let my pack scrape against the wall, the guard should have whirled and confronted me. He didn't, because he was dozing standing up. The Webley didn't have to speak. I had my knife handy, too. The lucky fellow died in his sleep. I waved to Joan. She rushed up to the portal, glanced down at the guard, and averted her eyes. There was a lot of blood, and it was still flowing.

The door was secured with a chain and lock. It was a careless job, since the chain was bolted to the door frame and passed through the loop handle of the door. One didn't need to break the chain – just pry the handle, secured by screws, off the door. The barrel of the dead guard's rifle did that easily. Joan stepped carefully over the blood as we entered.

It was a long warehouse, with crates of various kinds of munitions stacked in rows. We went to work immediately and wordlessly, we prying boards in crates and inserting charges, Joan inserting fusing mechanisms. Almost seven minutes were up when we had exhausted our charges and fuses. I tapped Joan and said, "Time for you to run. Get to the fence. I won't be far behind." She did as I said, and I start back down the row, activating the fuses. This was quick work, and I was almost back to the door when I heard the voice. It wasn't Joan's, and it was speaking German.

"You there. What are you doing here? And where's Helmut?" He was on time, but he wasn't supposed to be chatty. He was supposed to just walk by. This was a rare case of my luck abandoning me. Now poor Joan was standing midway to the fence, a dim figure in the darkened yard. The guard had a small torch, which he fumbled with and finally got to shine. Those early flashlights were not very illuminating, but he could see Joan well enough now. I'm not sure if he could determine her age, sex, or favorite colors, but he knew she wasn't Helmut. "Who are you? Where's

Helmut?" he repeated. She said nothing.

The nice thing about knowing that an explosion is imminent and nearby is that decision making is easy. We needed to run for it, and a few gun shots wouldn't be sufficient warning to bring the cavalry to the rescue of the munitions dump in time. No, the rescue brigade would probably be running with us. I guessed the sentry was holding his torch in his right hand. I aimed the Webley slightly to the right of it, and slightly higher. I fired twice. I heard a grunt and a yelp and I ran for Joan, who was still deciding on a course of action. "We have about a minute to get as far away as we can," I shouted. "Let's head for that ditch we crossed just before we got here." She didn't say a word, just followed me to the fence. We ripped some clothes getting through, rose, and ran through the dark. I tripped once, banged a knee, struggled, and she helped me up. She was like a gazelle, and seemed hardly to touch the ground. The ditch loomed before we anticipated it and we pitched in, gasping. Three gasps and the fireworks started.

The explosions lasted for forty five minutes or more. Some were longer or louder than others. Meanwhile, the building was burning brightly, so I suggested to Joan that we quit admiring our handiwork and use the extra light to help us navigate away from Dinant, toward France, and to a safe daytime hiding place. That's when I got yet another affirmation of my belief in the inevitability of unintended consequences.

Joan said, "Right now I feel more like doing sex than I ever have in my life." She gave me a pleading look.

"Hold that thought," I said, "for some nice fellow in France."

Chapter Eleven

Door to Door Service

I carried the lady too

She made me feel so blue

But a life like mine is always just on the edge

She knew where she had to go

And I had to make it so

But between us there hovered a very serious wedge

So the day that we had to part

Tore a hole right through my heart

But somehow I knew it surely was for the best

If I just let the lady go

With things she never could know

In the end she seemed to me like all of the rest

Sung to the tune of *O Sole Mio*, this song was a favorite of golfing great Bobby Jones. He performed it at the tee of the 10th hole in nearly every tournament in which he played. He often accompanied himself on the Jew's Harp.

***

I had long discarded the lantern, the last vestige of Tartaq. We mucked through the dark as well as we could. We followed the canals that laced rural Belgium, wading when possible to remain trackless and avoid bramble and tripping cobbles. That made for slow going, but we were relentless. I tried to set an example of ignoring fatigue and Joan understood that wordless lesson. Still, by dawn we had spent the last reserves of energy, and it was time to hide anyway. In a little hollow off a canal, one thick with sedges, we let our exhaustion overtake us. We didn't see the sun rise. In fact, we didn't even see noon.

I touched Joan's cheek to awaken her. Without opening her eyes, she said, "Don't." She sat up, looked at me, then looked away. Her face was expressionless. When I could see her eyes, they seemed to following some imaginary humming bird. I could only imagine what the events of the preceding night had done to her mind, and I felt ashamed of myself. By that time I had been through so many harrowing experiences, so many battles, had rendered so many corpses to the earth, had performed so many death marches and narrow escapes, that I only needed to see if I was still breathing and hadn't too many holes in my skin to be thankful I was still there. This poor girl/woman was just realizing the world she had entered, and she wasn't sure she could cope. She needed some therapy, and I was never good at that. I knew what the matter was, so I asked, "What's the matter?" Do therapists think like courtroom lawyers, and never ask a question to which they don't know the answer? I don't know the answer to this question I just asked. Be that as it may, Joan said nothing, so I just let her stare off into nowhere while I reached into the bag to fetch some edible roots. I had also saved one last bottle of wine, in case a celebration would be in order, so I dug out the cork and offered her a root and a swig. "Take this. You need it."

She ignored me as if I weren't there. I thought perhaps she was entering some sort of shock, which caused me to start listing remedies and options. The trouble was, I didn't know the remedies and the options varied from callous to cruel. So I did nothing but wait. She finally turned toward me. I'm saw tears in her eyes and that buoyed my spirits. Crying means one isn't emotionally bankrupt. There are feelings in there some place. She said, "I'm sorry."

I ignored what was a groundless apology. "You should eat," I said. "We have a long way to safety."

"Did you not hear me?" she asked.

"I heard something about sorry. I'm not sure what that applies to."

"Everything I've done. Trusting Tartaq. Exposing myself to the guard at Dinant. Dragging you back on this escape. Twice I've tried to distract you with sex. I've done nothing right."

"You have it backwards. You've done nothing wrong. We're this far because you got us here. And before we leave here tonight, to head toward Champagne, you will set our course."

"You don't think badly of me? Don't think me wanton? Or insentient?"

"I think you're a brave woman and a good person. And I'm counting on you to continue to be my guide."

She fell silent again, pondering. The shock, or whatever it was, seemed gone. I felt lucky again, even though she didn't speak for more than hour. Then, with some resolve, she said, "Do you think I might go up to the top of the berm so that I might look around? I think I can find a landmark to set our course."

"Let me go with you. We can crawl up there, and two of us can make doubly sure it's safe to stand up and look around."

We did exactly that. After we stood, it took but a few moments for Joan to regain aplomb. "See that mountain, there?" She pointed at a bump in the landscape.

"You mean that little hill?"

"You've flown over much of Belgium. We call that a mountain. In fact, we call it Rat Mountain. All the 'little hills' have their distinguishing features. I learned these from travels with my father. That's how I knew I could guide you. If we head almost due west and keep Rat Mountain on our right, we'll get to France very close to the Champagne District. It will have some lights on it at night. There is a hotel on top. The Boche are probably there now. I assume you know how to use the stars to keep us going west, and not circling Rat Mountain."

Yes, her confidence was back. Now she was challenging me. "Yes. I can do that."

"And handle getting through German lines, if it comes to that?"

"Yes. I can do that, too."

"Then let's go back down. I'm suddenly hungry."

I suppose she was no more emotionally volatile than most females. In truth, I like that about women. I can't think of many things I don't like about women. Damn this immortality shit.

Chapter 12

It Had to be Done

If you sell your body

Do you sell your soul

The whore in me asks all the time

If you sell your soul

Do you sell your body

The whore in me laughs all the time

You do what you do

And make what you can

The whore of the gods knows the game

And if someone gets hurt

If someone gets killed

They've only themselves to blame

The origin of this is uncertain. It was found on a scrap of crumpled paper Shakespeare's janitor turned up while cleaning house. It was during the period when the bard was writing *Macbeth,* although one shouldn't attach any significance to that fact.

***

We made our way virtually unmolested for about two nights. We even stole a chicken from the front yard of a farmhouse. The sun was up and everyone was in the field, so it wasn't particularly daring. In a secluded copse we roasted the bird for breakfast before we took our daily sleep. We needed that rest, because late that afternoon, shortly after we resumed our trek, we came in sight of the the German lines.

There were no trenches here. From our brushy observation post we could see a few artillery pieces, some trucks, and a tank. I knew the Germans didn't have any tanks in the field yet, to it must have been a captured British tank. Away from the trenches, this would have been a good place to test such a vehicle. The fields around the trenches were so pocked by artillery shells that tanks were just clumsy, often useless cannons, sitting ducks for the primitive anti-tank weapons of the time. There was a large tent, probably a command post, and shelter tents strung out on both sides of us. Joan said, "What do you think?"

"I think we have arrived at our last two major challenges."

"Two?"

"To get through the German lines, and to not get killed by soldiers of the Triple Entente. We don't look like reputable allies. We have to change rapidly and convincingly from saboteurs to refugees. Deadly one minute, submissive the next. We have to get it right on both ends, or all this travail is for naught."

"So, starting with the first: how do we do it?"

"We could try to go around, but I don't know how far the line extends. The longer we are in German territory, the greater the probability of getting caught, especially so close to a concentration of the enemy. A rough mathematical guess tells me that we're better off going straight through. At least, as straight as we can. I can't think of a more detailed plan than that until we get down there tonight and see what's between us and France. We won't know what the dance is until we hear the music. Like a good dance partner, you'll follow my lead."

"Yes. I will."

***

We had plenty of moon now, which was good for reconnoitering but bad for stealth. In the moonlight, moving slowly, silently, drifting toward our enemy, the whole scene assumed a dreamlike quality. It wasn't us, because we weren't aware of our bodies; only what we could observe, and we had no control over that. The objects, the men out there could be anything, morph to anything, anything we could imagine. At least this was my mindset, and I felt Joan was sensing in the same way. We had to shake this feeling, to regain control, to affirm that we weren't dreaming and the events would be of our making. I touched Joan gently, a finger to my lips, then whispered in her ear, "What do you see?" This made her realize she was awake and could organize the portrait before her. I pointed to my own ear and she understood.

In it she whispered, "They seemed to have given the tank a wide berth. And there is only one guard on the tank. He seems to be the only one up. And he's not moving."

I whispered back, "That's all good. There may be sentries down the line on either side, but I can't see any. I hope that means they wouldn't see us if we crossed the line here. The tank made a nice track for us to follow west if we haven't stirred the hornets' nest."

"What about the guard on the tank?"

"That will be your job. Take off your cap. Wipe dirt off your face. Look like the pretty girl you are. We'll test to see if he's sleeping. Walk right up to him, directly but quietly. If he doesn't stir, I'll follow. We'll be by him and down the track, and the first big obstacle is out of the way."

"And if he stirs?"

This was the tricky part, given what I was sure was Joan's still fragile psyche. "Take this." I handed her my knife. There might have been a bit of blood on it, from the door guard in Dinant. Blood or not, she shuddered when the grip hit her hand. "Talk to him. Make him think you're there because you are looking for a German boy. Get his back to me. When I come out of the brush he will turn to face me. His back will be to you. You're tall enough. With your left hand pull his head up. Then run the blade hard across his throat. He will die silently."

Even in the dark I could see the shock in her eyes, the revulsion in her face. "I can't. I've never…..I can't."

"We have been given a gift by providence. A single soldier between us and France. When he left his loved ones' arms, when you left your grandfather's care, neither one of you could know it would come down to this. Neither one of you would have wanted it so. But it has and it is. If you make me take care of this I'm certain we will get the entire German Army involved. And it won't turn out well for us. Are you ready to die after all we've done? Or worse? They'll execute me for sure. You they might save you for other things."

She leaned against the largest branch she could find. Her first few breaths were rapid, and I was afraid she was going to faint. But then she began to breathe more deeply, and her face hardened. She hugged me and stepped back. "Is there any reason we should wait?"

I took a deep breath myself. "No. The conditions will never be better."

Without another word, Joan stepped into the clearing, moving almost mechanically toward the tank. I would say instinctively, but I don't know where such instinct might have been acquired. Perhaps early in our species the female became aware that the survival of said species rested on her womb? For her, now, Joan and I were the whole of the species, and our survival was in her hands.

She got quite close to the tank before the guard, the only German in sight, stirred. He had been propped against those terrible metal treads, as if he were asleep. Perhaps he had been, since he suddenly jumped up to face her, seemingly startled. He started to level his gun at her, but she said something to make him hesitate. She spoke so softly I couldn't make out her words. It was something that had him confused. To my amazement, he put his weapon on the ground and touched her shoulder. I couldn't hear what he said, either, but the gesture was one of consolation. I was so absorbed by the scene I almost forgot my part. I stepped out into the open, rustling the bush just slightly. He turned toward the sound and peered through the moonlight, dimmed by high clouds. He could probably see a figure, perhaps that of a man. I moved a little, just enough to keep his attention.

Joan did her part then, expertly, as if she were a trained assassin. In one motion she put a hand on his forehead and ran the knife across his throat. When she let him go, he turned back to her. I'm sure his eyes were wide in disbelief, although I didn't see them. Joan broke his fall as he slumped to the ground, so there was hardly a sound. Then she looked at me. I was still absorbing what I had just seen. I had to shake myself into action. By running I reached her in a few seconds. I couldn't read anything in her face as I took the knife, sticky with blood, from her hand. "Let's leave," I said. "We're not done yet. The escape is only half over." I pulled gently on her arm.

"Wait," she said. She knelt down to the soldier, who was resting on his side. She pulled on his shoulder, so that we could see his face. She let out a little sob, and even I felt a catch in my throat. I doubt that the fellow was even eighteen. There was no hint of a beard, the skin was soft and new and very smooth. The innocent blue eyes were still wide open. I closed them.

As we stood, she said, "I told him my lover was a soldier in this camp. Could he help me find him. I wanted to give him one last kiss before we parted, perhaps forever." She looked down at the boy soldier. "And then I killed him."

She started to weep, so I embraced her and said close to her ear, "You may have your cry, but don't make this killing in vain. Cry as we run. We have to go. Now."

She didn't utter another word, merely following me as I began a trot down the tank track. The gibbous moon was free of the clouds now, so we had enough light to move fairly quickly. I made sure she could keep pace. She never quavered, and her expression never changed. She was breathing no harder than I. Fortunately our packs were almost empty, almost unnecessary. Now my problem became how far to run. We needed to be safely away from the Germans, but we didn't need to run pall mall into the French lines. Just after midnight, approaching a little stream, I called a halt. Joan heeded me, still wordless. Like me, she was sweating and breathing hard, but not exhausted. "It's time for water," I said. "And time to rest until daybreak."

I splashed some water from the stream, cupped my hands to drink, and motioned for her to do the same. Mechanically, she followed my lead. I helped her sit down on a soft spot on the bank and fished the few bits of food we had left out of the packs. I literally pushed some into her mouth, the voluntary opening of which her only acknowledgement of my efforts. I've already admitted that I am a lousy nurse. I realized that I was in a situation where even a good nurse might not do well. I wanted to shake her, to make her talk, to make her angry, perhaps to make her weep again. Then I wanted to talk, to cajole, to make light of the situation, or to make it verge on the catastrophic. I rejected talk, also. In my ineptitude, I decided to wait it out. I fashioned the packs into a pillow, and lowered her head to it. She didn't resist. I then took her in an embrace, just to keep her warm. Traveling at night had solved that problem up to now, but there would be no more traveling this night. Even in my embrace, Joan stared beyond me. I stayed still and quiet. Finally, she slept.

***

I awoke with a shove from Joan. She was pushing me away. Not in anger. She just wished to be free of me. I could understand that. My own muscles were sore from inaction and awkward positioning. We both stood and stretched. I tried to appear as if we were in a routine, taking another drink from the stream and splashing water on my face. "Now let's see if we can find some Frenchmen who believe we are friendly. And hungry. And looking for a place of safety."

There was a long pause, and as she slipped by me toward the stream, she said, "I think I hate you." Then she splashed water on her face and took a small drink. She turned back to me, expecting a response.

"Because I brought you into the middle of a battlefield? Because I mentored your first killing of another human being?"

"Because it all seems so easy to you. I was shocked when you killed old Tartaq, but I wasn't devastated. He was going to turn us over to the Boche, and it had to be done. I was shocked when I saw the guard at Dinant lying in a pool of his blood, but I still had some soul left, because he was between us and the assigned mission.

Can you imagine what I felt when I saw the boy you had me kill, what I felt before I lost all feeling? I can't ever get that part of me back, that ability to feel. I hate myself, and I hate you for making me hate myself. I feel wretched, because I truly am a wretch. A wretch like you, only you don't know you're a wretch."

I'm no therapist, but this I could talk about. "You may be right about me, for reasons you'll never know. I've been at this business for longer than I care to say. I've shot people and bombed people and strangled people and slashed people. I've never taken pleasure in it, I've never taken profit from it, and I've only done it when it was necessary to keep them from committing or abetting homicide themselves. I've tried to do it in a fair battle, but sometimes I've struck first, without warning. Yes, arguably I may be wretched, because this seems to be my lot, the thing I'm best at, and don't for a minute think I don't get weary of it. Just remember, it's my talent that has you in France, alive. I happen to think there is nothing after death, so if you got killed along the way you wouldn't care, since there would no longer be a you to give a damn. But your grandfather would be shattered, and, believe it or not, I would carry your ghost with me for the rest of my life." I paused, to see if she would argue. She just frowned. "You,' I continued, "on the other hand, aren't consigned to a plight like mine. You did what you did in order to survive, and there were only those two options. Kill or be killed. It does not make you a "wretch", it makes you a human animal. I will get you to a place where you can work to aid the cause of our allies, and do it without killing anyone."

Apparently she had paid some attention. "And you? What will you do if we get into friendly territory? Go back to shooting and bombing people?"

"Would you have me do something different?"

She cocked her head. "No. I guess not. It's war, and somebody has to shoot and bomb. It might as well be someone who is good at it." She was becoming rational, although I was sure she would have relapses into remorse. She just hadn't fallen completely off the cliff; she had dangled on the edge. She probably hadn't completely walked away. That's something I was considering doing, and I saw no harm and some good in telling her that. "Believe it or not, I have some unfinished business in this war. After I take care of that, I will no longer have my heart in it. I'm fairly certain that the Germans will ultimately give it up, with or without my contributions to their defeat. And that dead boy affected me as much as he affected you. It's not good to go into battle when you're motivated only by self-preservation. The surest way to fail at self-preservation is to make that your only goal. You need a cause, a battle cry, to carry you through. I have only one of those left, at least in this war."

"It is said this will be the war to end all wars."

"Not likely." I couldn't tell her that such a thing had been said a thousand times before. She was, at least for a while, out of her funk, and it wasn't a propitious moment to reflect on mankind's collective stupidity. It was however a propitious moment to get going. We still had to find some friends. As we started walking, finding friends reminded me of something I needed to broach with Joan. I didn't look at her when I asked, "Do you have some destination in mind once we reach safe territory? Some place you or your father or your grandfather would favor? Friends?"

She was looking forward also when she answered. "Not really. I was hoping you would help me out there. I suppose, after the way I cursed you, that's out of the question. I'll just…"

"You'll just nothing. I was afraid to offer refuge after what I've put you through. I do have something in mind. The place I'm headed, St. Chalon, would be ideal for you. Mons. Poindex is a good man and could find some work to keep you occupied. He is an important supporter in the fight, and has a radio man. Just like Fat One. He could radio Fat One to let your grandfather know you're safe. You might have to start out milking cows, but you'd be secure until this war ends and you can return to Bastogne. And I'll be around, waiting for my next mission, so you'll have a familiar face until you make better friends."

"I accept your invitation. As for friends, either anyone would be better, or there is no better. I just don't know how to think of you. No, I do. Very clearly. It's just that it's momentary. One minute I love you, the next I hate you. What's wrong with me?"

"Nothing that doesn't exist in all humans. We want to do the right thing. We just don't know what it is. So we do what pleases us, or helps us survive, or seems right at the time, or what someone we consider wise or blessed tells us to do. Some people hear voices that tell them what the right thing to do is. We call them crazy if the voices are only in their head. If the voice is a king or a czar or a pope we call the person who listens to him a hero. The trouble is, the voices, no matter where they come from, are almost always wrong. After you understand that you see that you might as well decide for yourself. You can be just as wrong without their help. Sometimes you're actually right, but it's fleeting, because what makes sense now won't make sense tomorrow. So don't worry about it. And don't worry about how you feel about me. Whatever you think of me is probably right. I'm your best dream and your worst nightmare. All men are, and in places where women are equal to men, all women are, too."

She thought about that for a bit. Then she said, "If you say you should decide for yourself what the right thing to do is, why are you waiting for your next mission? For someone else to tell you what's the right course of action for you?"

"Oh, I'm not waiting for orders. I already know what I'm going to do. I just need the airplane to do it in. That's why I'm going to St. Chalon. M. Poindex will tell the British High Command that I'm ready and waiting. I expect that will get everyone's attention. I just don't know how long delivery will take."

"The next mission you've decided on – what will it be?"

"I can't tell you. Let's just say it's unfinished business." After a few steps I said, "Our mission this morning, however, is simple. We just have to find a sentry that we don't have to kill to get what we want."

Denis De Luchi

Chapter Thirteen

Mother Delivers a New Baby

Oh, my Queen, my Mother

I take your schilling

In the form of a child

A brother

He will be my friend

My comrade

We will soar together

Or fall together

He hasn't your blue blood

Like me, his blood runs purple

Which one of your many lovers

Sired the both of us

Eleanor of Aquitaine received this message, delivered by a black dove. Since she had born at least six bastard children in various convents, she never found out who wrote it.

***

In the end, our entry into French territory wasn't dramatic. We were wandering down a dirt road through a small forest when we encountered a young guard manning a sentry post. He was more a militia man than a soldier, so the French apparently didn't worry about a horde of Huns pouring down this particular highway. The young man was much more interested in Joan than me, and any difference in dialect was overcome by careful attention to her explanation of our presence. He would be glad to help. I don't think he noticed our sudden sadness when we looked closely at him. His cherub face was just like that of the German soldier whose throat Joan had cut. He was somewhat shocked when, after he had agreed to lead us to his headquarters, a tearful Joan fell on him with tears and kisses. He didn't understand when she cried, "Oh, God, I'm so sorry. I'm so sorry."

***

We bumped along in the back of a military truck, Joan learning against me, her eyes still moist. We had had spent two days verifying our loyalty and use to the allies, with radio calls to M. Poindex, who gave a close enough physical description of me to convince the French captain I was in fact an escapee from occupied Belgium. They had accepted Joan almost immediately, since she looked so sad and angelic. We ate in the mess a hall and slept in a corner of the barracks, with essentially no privacy for poor Joan. It was made worse by the fact that almost all the soldiers looked like the man she had killed, so she teared-up constantly. The only times she left her cot were for the dining hall and the outhouse. At least she had a semi-private outhouse, using the hole dug for the officers. All this is why she was still teary-eyed in the truck. Conversation with her was cursory to nil. The truck seats were hard wood and the ride was jarring, but I don't think Joan noticed.

The truck dropped us at a little *moulin*, which resided at a T in the road. The truck turned north. We headed south, walking toward St. Chalon. I don't know if it was the fresh air or just my company; whatever it was, Joan started to brighten. I began to whistle *Frere Jacques,* and she picked it up with a hum, in round. That was enough to make even a crusty cynic feel a moment of joy.

***

M. Poindex was absolutely ebullient. As Joan watched he hugged and kissed me, exclaiming over and over, "I knew it, I knew it. I knew you would make it." When I finally settled him down, I introduced him to Joan. "Ah," he said, "so you were the partner in the fireworks in Dinant. It was all over the intelligence network. You can't count the number of boys who will live for lack of German bullets and cannon shells. You two are heroes, and you a mere girl. How brave you are!" He started to get emotional again, so I had to remind him that the mere girl had walked a long way, besides blowing up a munitions dump and living off the land. I left out any killing, which I would discuss out of her presence when I briefed him on how she needed to be treated. He put his arm around her. "You must forgive me, my dear. I was so happy to see the Duke I forgot your proximate needs. Of course you are fatigued. Come into the house, and we will get you settled."

As we followed him I said, "And me? I don't want to be settled. I want another airplane, just like the one I lost. I'm ready to go back to work."

He stopped and turned with a smile. He waited, taking some deep breaths as the smile broadened. "Oh, it makes me even happier to hear that. And for the news I have to give you. Your command has built you another, even better airplane. Someone named Leplombe has been working on it since before you flew off with his first one. I will radio them tonight, and by the gods you'll have it a few days. You and I will, as you say, be back in business."

***

After I explained the reasons for the fragility of Joan's psyche to Poindex, he agreed she needed rest, then light work to occupy body and mind, and some new friends who were her age and not hardened by combat. That night he established contact with Fat One, so that The Pisser would know his granddaughter was safe. I imagine The Pisser went on a real pissing spree that night, but not so much that the Germans could detect his urine in their wine. For two days I had some pleasant, innocuous chats with Joan, and even then I could sense that her mind was releasing the tension that pulled it from sorrow to self-loathing and back again, passing through the mid-point of love and hate for me. It would take a while; a few milked cows, a few laughs with her contemporaries, especially with girls who didn't look like young German soldiers.

***

I paced, sometimes impatiently, sometimes enjoying the grassy smell and the puffs of clouds against the blue, around the pasture M. Poindex had allotted as an airfield. Before we went out there, he had shown me the ordnance my new machine would carry. A thousand rounds of 30 caliber for the twin Vickers. Two actual fin stabilized bombs, aimable in a dive.

"Are you sure?" I asked. "I can't imagine such a load, weighing nearly as much as the machine itself."

"That's what they have told me. And that's why I have a barn full of machine gun ammunition and bombs. Believe me, I am uncomfortable with such a store. It makes my little farm a target, just like the one you destroyed in Dinant. Fortunately, I don't think the Boche have any idea what we do here, other than milk cows and grow some grains."

"That means I never led any back here during my first operations. I promise you, I will be just as careful again. So far, we've been careful and maybe a little lucky. I kept the Smilloux brothers out of the spotlight, I kept you out of the spotlight, and kept myself and my airplane in it. We'll do it again." I didn't tell Poindex that I wouldn't be around much longer. I just needed to terrorize the German lines enough to get Von Richthofen to come out and play. I was planning the last chapter of the Purple Duke. That doesn't count the original Purple Duke, who will never be forgotten, because he really was purple. I just had a purple airplane. Or would it still be purple? My impatience grew.

Just after three o'clock we could make out a speck above the horizon. It grew bigger and more discernible, until we could see it was a bi-plane, and, after another few minutes, it was purple. Yet another few minutes later, we could hear its engine. Barely. It was the smoothest hum I had heard from an airplane engine to that point in my life. The very low growl spoke of precision and power. I was already blessing Leplombe and the damn thing hadn't even landed.

When it did, I was sure I had been projected years in the future. I suppose I had. This was no modified Nieuport 17. Oh, there might have been that lineage hidden somewhere in that airframe, but it was covered by Leplombe's genius. When I think of my negative first impression of the man, compared to the way I came to revere him, I confirm my vow to never not like a man until he gives me reason not to like him. This business of prejudice is so complicated. I would have been stunned by Newton's genius, but if I got to know him personally I probably wouldn't have liked him. What does that all mean? Don't ask me. Anyway, Leplombe was a nice guy, and a helluva aeronautical engineer.

The plane. From the moment the ferry pilot taxied up, I could see and hear the future. The engine, though still a radial, neither shook nor belched the slightest smoke. In front of the Vickers was some sort of small intake, probably providing extra push for a supercharger. The exhaust ports were smaller than usual, and faired back. The lower wings where bigger than the standard Nieuport, while the struts between the wings were smaller and of a different design. The control surfaces were slightly larger both in width and length. The rudder look made to handle the torque of a much more powerful engine, and the propeller, when unwound to a stop, showed three blades instead of two. Below each Vickers there was an access door, obviously to load ammunition, on the ground, just the once. The Vickers themselves were recessed into the top of the fuselage, instead sitting on mounts in front of the pilot. The windshield started just aft of their apertures and sloped steeply toward the cockpit. I guessed this was for streamlining. I also guessed that the small airscoops I had noticed were for cooling the barrels of the Vickers. It turns out I was guessing correctly.

When the engine had stopped, the ferry pilot jumped out. He looked at Poindex and then at me. Poindex still had his Dali face hair and a paunch. His face showed his years. I was fit and young – at least I looked young. The ferry pilot said to me, "Are you the lucky bastard who gets to take this beauty into combat?" I nodded and extended my hand. As he shook it, he said, "She just loves to fly, and is as obedient as a well-trained dog."

"Yes, I'm the lucky bastard. Alan Roderick."

He looked me over. "You mean, the Purple Duke. I'm Jeremy Phillips."

"That too, I suppose. This is Mons. Poindex. Gentleman farmer and patriot. He provides all the support I need."

Phillips nodded. He was tall, thin, and very young. Why did I keep seeing the youth of the combatants? Why was I beginning to feel a grudge against the old, brandy swilling generals who sent a generation off to war from the comfort of some plush headquarters? Phillips was cheerful, though. "I'm very pleased to meet you, Mons. Poindex."

So cheerful. He hadn't killed anyone yet, or felt the death of comrades around him. Maybe he would remain a ferry pilot, and not have to smell the trenches, or the smoke, or the gas. That wasn't up to me, however. The proper use of the purple airplane he had just delivered was. "You must be tired, Jeremy. Have you flown all the way from Glaston Priory?"

"It was quick and easy in this machine. A delight."

"Still, you'll want to rest a night before you start back. Mons. Poindex can make you quite comfortable."

Jeremy shuffled his feet. "Actually…..yes, I'll stay the night, but….could I ask an enormous favor?"

"Of course you can ask. We'll break out the best wine, but if you want a Paris whore you'll have to go there and ask in person."

"No, what I want is not to have to take ground transport back to Calais. Could you possibly fly me? In this?" He indicated the purple beauty.

I only thought for a second. "Why not? In fact, it's a grand idea. We can stuff you behind the cockpit, and I can get a feel for the airplane with the first fellow to fly it looking over my shoulder. Let's celebrate tonight, and I'll take you to Calais in the morning."

Poindex was more than game. "Yes, indeed, I will break out the best wine. And the best brandy I have. We can get old Perrier to play the squeeze box and we'll have a dance. I'm sure the young ladies who work here would be glad to join in."

Phillips' eyes were glowing. I was sure he was thinking, *isn't war a grand adventure.* I, on the other hand, was more jaded. I looked at M. Poindex, the boss of the place, and thought, *Hail, Caesar! We who are about to die salute you.* I couldn't say that out loud, though.

***

Poindex's idea was a good one. As soon as word spread there was a general air of festivity around the farm. People who should have been harvesting soy beans or baling hay were instead busy preparing one of the barns for dancing duty. There were hums and smiles all around, less than a thirty minute airplane ride from bullets and cannons. We now know that anticipation of a brief moment of pleasure dumps all the stress producing chemicals out through the bladder. Or the liver. Or whatever. The tension of war was momentarily relieved.

I sought out Joan and found her sweeping the barn floor. She had a beautiful smile for me, so I was on the good side of her yin/yang thoughts of me. "You disappeared into the work force more rapidly than I anticipated," I said.

"They've been very kind to me. And I needed to get busy as soon as possible. It's the best cure for sadness and depressing thoughts."

"That's so true. All my life I've found the best way not to feel down is to work up......a sweat."

She laughed. "I hear this was your idea."

"No. It was purely Poindex. But that reminds me. Surely you haven't worked up an attachment to a farm hand this quickly. At least I hope you haven't."

"Why? Are you asking me to the dance?"

"No. I will attend stag and tap my feet for the woman I love in England. But I do have someone in mind for you."

"Now you are a big brother."

"Not quite, considering what I'm about to suggest."

"What's that?"

"Well, the fellow who delivered my airplane is spending the night. Lieutenant Phillips. He's a handsome guy. Bright and enthusiastic. I thought you might pair up with him."

"That's a true big brother. It sounds perfectly nice."

"Here's the point. When I said 'enthusiastic' I meant anxious to get into this war. I understand that feeling. I've had it several times myself. Looking at it from my present perspective, I just worry that he's going to try things that will have a good chance of getting him killed. This might be his last party."

"So I should be cheerful and even flirtatious?"

"More than that. Remember when you said you felt amorous, just after we blew up the munitions plant? You wanted sex right then. And I said to save that thought for a lucky fellow at a later date. This is the date."

"I see now why you said 'not quite'. That's not what a big brother would tell his little sister. To go open herself to a man, just to give him a fond memory."

"Don't be angry with me. This isn't like telling you to kill someone." I was sorry the second I uttered that last sentence, but she seemed amused.

"I'm not angry. I'm flattered that you think I could make an important contribution to the war. I may just do that. And I'd probably like it."

***

Phillips was even more cheerful than the day before as I tucked him behind the cockpit. "It appears you enjoyed yourself last night. I saw you dancing with my friend Joan."

"Yes, sir. She was a most gracious young lady. She says you recommended me to her. I'm very grateful. We intend to correspond."

I didn't want further intelligence on the subject. I had noted that they left together before Perrier stopped providing music, so I assumed they did more dancing in private. That, of course was their affair. All I said was, "I'm glad you hit it off."

Phillips let the subject go, but he wasn't through thanking me. "It's so good of you to do this," he said. "I want to get back as soon as possible. They are forming a new squadron and I don't want to miss out. We'll be flying Camels. Not as sprightly as this plane, but good enough to battle the Hun."

"So, how did you get the ferry job? It's my turn to thank you for delivering her so quickly and in such perfect shape."

"We had a kind of fly-off in the Camels. I won."

"That means you're a good pilot. Don't let that make you an incautious one. I know you're anxious for combat, but let a person who has been there give you some advice. Your opponents will be skilled, too, and they will have plans and practice to maximize their effectiveness. You must do the same thing. You must be confident, not because you won a fly-off, but because you use your considerable skills with intelligence. Go through a battle in your mind, then practice until certain tactics become instinctive. Never take anything for granted, expected the unexpected, and imagine thoroughly enough so that the unexpected becomes a very small set. You should be thinking, 'What will I do if....'" every night, in the mess hall, at the bar. Trade ideas with your comrades. You can never be too smart, too prepared. Learn the favorite tactics of the German aviators. Live it." I had to stop myself. I was beginning to sound like I should be in a pulpit.

He took it good faith. "Thank you very much for that advice, sir. I will do my best to follow it."

I was glad to hear that. I really didn't want him to die in combat.

***

On the way to Calais I did some simple toying with the controls and engine settings. The weather was good and the plane was fast. When I dropped him off, the farewells were short. He was already scrambling for a ferry. I did a few tricks on the way back, things I might try in combat. Even with the extra time it took to practice dive bombing and going from near stall to max speed, I was back before dark. What a super airplane that was.

Denis De Luchi

Chapter Fourteen

First Things First

I carved a little gargoyle

I thought it was so cute

But it scared the little children

They saw evil at the root

I brought to my lover

Surely she would see

What I meant by all my carving

It would show no bad in me

But my loved one seemed confused

Are you saint or are you devil

Is the figure for protection

Or is Hell your own true level

So I cast aside the gargoyle

For it truly was confusing

I created a machine gun

That is so much more amusing

Written by the famous self-flagellant Saint Oscar of Moscow on April 13, 1140 C.E. Two days later he beat himself to death.

***

"Maximize the ordnance, Poindex. I'm going hunting."

M. Poindex smiled at me. "I will give you a little something for everything you might spot. Although, if I know you, you have just one specific quarry in mind. And that you must find by random chance."

I watched old Perrier, the accordion player, attaching bombs, one under each wing. He had already taught himself how to load the ammunition for the new- fangled recessed Vickers machine guns. He had them primed and ready. "If I wreak enough havoc in the trenches and with German airplanes, I won't have to rely on chance," I said

"You'd better watch out. The men on the ground have become familiar with airplanes as war machines by now. They have dedicated gunners shooting at you, men who have practice with moving targets. I've heard the men in the trenches fire at airplanes just for the fun of it. Sometimes their own airplanes. So now you have to expect bullets from the ground as well as the sky. And the ones on the ground have nothing to do but shoot their gun. They are all nice and stationary and secure. You must have many skills, some all at once. These gunners need only one skill, and maybe a little brandy to sip on, if their officers have any sense."

"It's only fair. I'll be coming at them with bullets and bombs, soaring while they sit. Why shouldn't they be able to shoot back?"

"Does that mean you want me to pack some brandy in the cockpit for you? To even things up?"

"No. I'll wait until I get back to enjoy that. You see, that's another advantage I have over them. Tonight, if I live, I'll sleep between sheets in a comfortable bed in your house. They'll still be in those stinking trenches."

"Then at that time we'll drink to the fact that you're still alive."

"Do me a favor. If I don't come back from one of these missions, do drink a toast."

"To you?

"If you wish. Better to the living. To Joan and old Perrier and yourself. I won't much give a damn if it comes to that point. Whatever makes you feel good."

"Well, my friend, good luck. One mission at a time."

***

That first time out I ran across no German airplanes, and none of the ground shooters came anywhere close to hitting my purple beauty. The airplane was so quick, or they were so confounded by the unexpected return of the Purple Demon, that few of them shot, and those that did missed widely. I returned the favor by missing the tanks I tried to dive bomb, and I mean missing badly, at least on the first one. On the second I was close, close enough to confirm that I had reasoned out the method for very accurate dive bombing. It required being in an almost vertical dive, siting the target as I would with the guns, a releasing the bomb just before I pulled up. The release had to be before I changed direction, but only a second or so before. I didn't want to be flying alongside the bomb toward the target. It was the bomb that had to hit the target, not me, but I had to get close enough to ensure a high probability of success.

The easy part was shooting up the enemy trenches. Those Vickers were responsive for all thousand rounds, and I think I put all thousand down a couple of those large slits in the ground. I tried not to think about the fact that there were people in those slits, and in little flashes my hand would try to jerk away from the trigger. In those flashes I saw children running around the in the trenches, little boys in short pants, little girls in pigtails. There were only a few such flashes that first time out in the new Purple Demon, and they only lasted for a fraction of a second each time, but I knew they wouldn't stay away. I would have to live with them until I could end this thing in my own way.

***

On the second day I paid more attention to the ground fire, because there were still no German airplanes to be seen. The gunners were still missing. It might have been my imagination telling me they were missing by less. I tore up the trenches again. In the little flashes, slightly more persistent, I recognized some of the little children – they were faces from my childhood in Scotland, almost ninety years before. There had been so many adventures since then, so many romances, so many exposures to violence that I thought they had been buried irretrievably deep under the detritus of life. In little flashes they emerged, then went away as I concentrated on the strafing run and bullets coming in my direction. I didn't want them hanging around in my mind, but I couldn't seem to evict them.

On the third mission day the men who manned the guns were no longer stupefied by the Purple Demon. They were just pissed off. I had just felt the thud of a couple of hits, their first, when I saw the Albatross D – II's. Two of them in loss formation, and it was obvious they were coming for me. Finally. The German High Command had finally believed the reports of the return of the purple airplane; it was probably the damage assessment of my efforts that got their attention. I was offended that it was only a couple of old Albatrosses. They should have sent their best.

The air battle was short. The German pilots employed their usual tactics: the leader taking me on one side, his wingman waiting on the other. My own ship was so much better than theirs that any tactic was futile. I pushed the throttle to the firewall, went into a vertical climb while they watched, rolled over and down on the lead, and let the Vickers blow away the entire empennage. As he went down I rolled toward the wingman, pulled up and looped behind him. I'm sure I had more airspeed at the start than he thought possible, because he made no evasive maneuvers whatsoever. I was on his tail, which he didn't have for very long. This had to be observed by everyone on the ground, which was my intention. I hoped to keep their radio waves busy.

The fourth and fifth days went much the same. The Germans were sending their pilots down to my territory for me to use as target practice. Since no one with air experience survived to brief them on my capabilities, they had to rely on reports from ground observers, who couldn't possibly give expert analyses of the action. By the fifth day I had stopped strafing. On the day before, I had jettisoned my bombs when the air opponents appeared, so I had stopped loading bombs, also. The most troubling aspect of this development was that, because the air battles were so easy, the faces of childhood friends flashed more vividly, transferred from the trenches to the cockpits I was destroying. I needed the Germans to get it. I wanted to fight the best. For my sanity, for the salvation of my humanity, I had to fight the best.

***

It was just a week after I started my rampage that the red Fokker tri-planes showed up. It's funny. That morning, Poindex had been almost adamant. "You really should load the bombs. Just the two direct hits you got on tanks have destroyed a lot of confidence in those tank crews."

"No. I have a feeling about today. I think my message has been received." Of course, I was right.

It was a formation of six. I presumed von Richthofen was the leader. From the way they broke it was obvious they had no idea of the vastly superior performance of the purple beast. They were about to take me on using their usual tactics. I couldn't ask for more. I called on full power and was able to gain a perch before they could react. Two had already run off to my starboard. I rolled toward them, letting the nose drop to gain even more speed, pulled up, rolled over onto my back, and caught them sideways. I had them broadside, lined up in my gunsight. Two short bursts from my inverted airplane and they were out of the battle. I went to a ninety degree bank to my left. Over my head I could spot the leader and his three remaining wingmen. I was still at max power, so I skidded the nose straight up and hung on my prop. It took all my controls to maintain that posture for a few seconds. The wingmen, two of whom were already some distance from the lead, spread out further. I dropped the nose and went after the most distant two. They started to turn into me but I could outrun their turn. When I caught them broadside once again I went vertical, rolled, went inverted, and had them in my sights. Ducks in line. It only took one burst to destroy both.

Now the lead, whom I hoped was von Richthofen, had just one wingman. I can't say that I actually saw it, but that wingman turned away from the battle. The lead had waved him off. It had to be von Richthofen. He was saying, "I am the best. This is my fight."

By this time von Richthofen had to know how much my plane could outperform his. He was a knight with guns for a sword and skill for armor, all still intact, but on a mount that was a donkey, pitted against an opponent astride a magnificent war horse. He would have to count on his armor to bear him through, until he could use his sword. Yes, he had to know. He would probably lose. He pulled down his face plate and readied his sword.

I chased him all over the sky. He turned harder than anyone I had yet seen, he rolled faster than I thought that Fokker could. I was afraid he'd break the wings off before I caught him the way I wanted. He must have been surprised when he discovered my airplane was not only faster, it could turn with him. He must have been even more surprised when he tried to make me overrun him and I could slow almost to stall very rapidly. Leplombe had install something new, something Lieutenant Phillips had shown me with great excitement, something which would later be called airbrakes, but which Leplombe had named reverse controls.

No matter what he did, no matter what tricks he tried, some of which I had never seen before, I stayed with him, or pulled up and away to watch. I've never been fully able to express my admiration for the man, a man defeated from the start, who couldn't stop trying to win. It was clear: if he couldn't win he would accept glory in defeat. He would force me to finish it. Sometimes I wonder how it would have ended if I didn't have such a superior machine.

But the kill wasn't what I was after. I wanted a different kind of victory. It was personal, not between me and von Richthofen, but between me and the war. The Germans were the enemy. Unfortunately, the British had become the enemy too. Oh, not the poor bastards in the trenches. No, the people in high places on both sides who had gone to war because they could. They could marshal cannons and ships and planes and machine guns, and they could marshal the fodder to feed these things. I saw no victory for them, and I would feel no victory in shooting down von Richthofen.

Finally, he tired. He rolled wings level and slowed to a comfortable speed. The tricks were done, his guns never fired. I pulled up alongside him, pointed to a pasture we were passing and motioned for him to land. He nodded understanding. The last time we did this, he had had the upper hand. I'm sure he was already wondering what was going to happen. I had to appear somewhat unpredictable to him. One thing was clear – I hadn't made the kill. Was I returning a favor?

***

He was already out of the cockpit and standing beside the red tri-plane when I taxied up. He appeared unarmed, but I had my Webley out, just in case. It wasn't necessary. He was quite composed. As I climbed from the cockpit he said, "I had a feeling we'd meet again."

"I wasn't so sure," I admitted. "At least, not at first. I didn't know what I wanted. I was just glad to have escaped and destroyed that prototype airplane. Somewhere along the way back my thoughts crystallized. I wanted to battle you again."

"This time with an even better aircraft. That's a marvelous machine. It would take me some time to learn how to beat you in it. Obviously, I didn't have that time today." He stopped talking for a moment and frowned. Then came the thought uppermost in his mind. "It gave you the ability to not have to end it honorably. I would have preferred to have it finish in the air." Then, as if in debate with himself, he said, "Although I see why you've done what you've done. You wanted to even the score."

"Something like that."

"In any case, I'm now your prisoner. Do you plan to march me to some French village and have the little authority there jail me?"

"No."

"What, then? Are you going to shoot me?" He nodded toward my Webley.

I was embarrassed and tucked the gun back under my arm. "Not that, either."

"You're a strange fellow. You seem to make up the rules as you go along. War has rules, you know. Especially among us airmen. You broke one when you refused to capitulate after I forced you down in my territory. You have reciprocated, and I won't break that rule. You won fair and square, although I still think I could beat you in equal airplanes."

"I won't argue, because we'll never know."

"How do you know I won't escape, or be otherwise repatriated to fly again for Prussia?"

"That's moot, because I don't intend to make you a prisoner. We won't meet again because I'm quitting this foolishness. Not the combat against you. The whole war."

He showed genuine surprise. "What?! You would desert your service? I don't take you for a coward. So I must take you to be mad."

"I am mad. As in angry. I'm fed up with this greater madness called war. I've come to the point where I don't care who wins, because it will be a hollow victory, and it won't solve anything. At the start, I wasn't sure which side to join, but the Habsburgs wronged me and I was born in Scotland, so I pledged myself to the Alliance. I could never claim to be a righteous person, but I have a great deal more humanity than the leaders on either side of this thing. I no longer want any part of it."

"And will you just walk into your commander's office and say, 'I quit?' Don't they have some rules about that in the Royal Flying Service? Especially for the person to whom they gave the best airplane in the world."

"Yes, they have rules about desertion. Funny. It's the 'best airplane in the world' that will allow me to override those rules. It will fly me away."

He shook his head in disbelief. "You'll never be able to do that. They'll never stop searching for you if you try."

I let that hang there for a minute. Then I said, "I can if you're willing to help me. It would mean putting a dent in that shield of honor you hold dear, it would mean dissembling, but it would be for the right reasons. And it would keep you out of a military prison."

"The right reasons?"

"Yes. To help a man who has done his duty faithfully, who has victories in the air and on the ground, and who can no longer, in all conscience, continue to do those duties. The second reason? To return yourself to the struggle, to those air battles you prize, without having to deal with the Purple Beauty here." I patted my plane.

Now he was focused. "You're serious. And you have a plan?"

We were face to face, now not three feet apart. "Yes. It will let me leave you to this war, which will probably kill you. You give so many people so many chances. Look at my airplane." I pointed to the several bullet holes in the fuselage. "Those didn't come from one of your pilots. They came from the ground. For all I know, my own people made them. There is no reason to expect a man in the trenches to be an expert at aircraft identification. In the smoke of the battlefield, in the dawn or dusk, with just a quick glance in the direction of the engine whine, a man might not distinguish between purple and red, might not see the black cross or the red, white, and blue circle. I'm fairly certain it was a German gunner because of where I was, but it doesn't matter. A man staggering of the edge of mud deep enough to drown him, a man thinking about his rotten feet and the dead comrade next to him, a man with a gun, will shoot it. And they're getting better. Look at the holes. I hope you don't die in this war. That's because I hope no one else dies in this war. It's a vain hope. If you do die, I hope it is through the skill of another pilot. The odds are, it won't be. It will be a lucky shot by a threadbare Australian sergeant who will never know he killed you, let alone who you were."

Von Richthofen wore a thin smile. "I appreciate your concern for me. You shouldn't bother. If I die in battle it will be honorable, no matter who makes the shot. That's not the question. The question is, 'what is your plan?'"

"My plan is to bid you on your way and return to my base for fuel. From there, I will disappear. No farewells. For them, I will be going back to war again today. They will never see me again."

"Surely there will a search. A confirmation of your demise or of your desertion."

"And that's where I need your help. You will be the confirmation that I was shot down."

"I will not lie for you, and I would never claim a victory I didn't achieve."

"You don't have to do either. You only need tell snippets of the truth. You're sure I was hit by ground fire. That's true, since I've shown you the holes. And you saw me fly off. Which, if you let me leave first, will also be true. And you saw me going down, because you were standing here when I just now landed. Another truth, although you won't add the last part. You don't claim the victory, and you don't know where I might have landed or crashed. Again, all unequivocal." I let him think about this for a moment. Then I said, "Surely it wouldn't stain your honor to enable a man to disengage himself from a war he truly believes to be fruitless, immoral, and nothing but tragic. A man who, up to this point, has been loyal to his duties, and now must be loyal to his heart.

He considered me. "Tell me, my strange friend, does this mean you will never again enter into a war on any side?"

"Never is a very long time. Longer for me than for you, although I can't tell you why that is. I can't hope to predict my future. I only know how I feel now. How very strongly I feel about this."

"Where do you plan to go?" He considered. "Wait. That's a foolish question. I shouldn't have asked and I really don't want to know. If you say are quitting the war, I believe you. You are a man possessed by an overwhelming and honest passion. I can sense that." He considered again. "You are going to refuel after we've already met. Will my testimony still seem true?"

"The chronology will be lost in the ether. I will tell them I have a date to meet you in a showdown. No one will know that we had our meeting before I told them it was going to happen. The lie is mine, which I don't mind. Among the lies I've told in my time, it's one of the most innocuous. All your testimony remains true." Before he answered I added, "I don't know about this passion business. I've never been a passionate man. However, about this I do feel very deeply."

Von Richthofen leaned against his plane. "It's strange. One lives his life by a code. It is a personal religion, demanding more devotion than an institutional one. Decisions should be easy if one adheres to one's code. Yet.....situations arise which can call forth mutually contradictory interpretations of the meaning of simple vows. This incongruity is emphasized by your own strangeness. I must believe your sincerity, and since I will make no lies or false claims of victory, in conscience I can choose to aid you. That means I trust you to have the integrity and ability to make good your disappearance. I trust that I will never see you again."

"You don't know how many people I have left in just this way."

"Since I will never fully understand you, or the meaning of what you've just said, I'll simply bid you farewell." Von Richthofen made a little bow of the head.

"We'll never know who was best. I don't care, and you shouldn't either. Just remember – airplanes aren't your only enemy. Bullets can come from below, too."

Now with a wave he said, "Like you, I do what I do. Good luck to you."

"And you."

Chapter Fifteen

In from the Cold

I've always liked the bumpy roads

You know you're goin' places

You don't know what's around the bend

And you're holdin' eights and aces

You might not make the curve, my friend

You might drive off the cliff

But you're hangin' on to one sure thing

Your life is never 'if'

This was an early Western ballad, written and performed by perhaps the most famous rodeo clown of all time, One Legged Juan Wombach. The tune is a continuous repetition of the first four notes of Beethoven's Fifth.

***

"Maximize the ordnance, Poindex. I'm going hunting."

He recognized those exact words from the first time I said them that day. After opening the ammunition panels he said, "It looks like you haven't used all the bullets this time out."

"There's a reason for that,' I said. "Reload the max, plus bombs. I have a date with von Richthofen, and I want to flash my sword first."

His eyes were big. "Von Richthofen? You tangled with him? And you both survived? And you have arranged a rematch? How?"

"Hand signals. There was too much interference this time. Too many on the ground shooting at both of us. Look at the holes." I nodded toward the rear of the fuselage.

"I can patch those, too, before you go."

"Never mind those. Just the guns and the bombs, and a full load of fuel. I'll drop the bombs before we tangle, but the battle may take a while. We're going to settle this away from the front, man to man, airplane to airplane."

For the first time I saw real concern on Poindex' face. "Are you sure you want to do this? I know this airplane will outfly the Fokker, and you are a truly good pilot. But the Red Baron is the Red Baron. A single victory might be good for your ego, but it isn't worth the risk of losing you and this airplane."

"There's no choice. When I devised the silly name, the Purple Duke was born. This has to be."

He shrugged. "The plane will be ready in an hour. Less."

"Oh. Please throw some wine and cheese into the cockpit pouch."

A smile and a nod.

I started to walk away, then was held by a thought. "While you're at it, could you find one of those smoke bombs you made and never seemed to have any use for? Strap it behind the cockpit, with a cord attached, so that the pin can pulled by the pilot."

"What good is a smoke bomb?"

"Sometimes they're a good ruse. An opponent might get careless if he thinks one is damaged." *Or, I might not need von Richthofen to testify to my demise.*

"Very clever."

"See you soon."

***

I sought out Joan. The girls in the barn said she'd gone to the house. Poindex had given her a small room of her own on the second floor. She was there.

She was surprised to see me. "Through with the war for the day?" At times the bitterness, the depression showed through. Probably only with me now. Her new friends seemed to cheer her, make her forget.

"No. I'm going out again." Her face fell. "I just wanted to let you know. It's a little rougher out there now. I may have to land someplace else. Continue the fight from there. If I don't come back, don't worry. I'm probably back in Belgium with your grandfather and the Smelly Boys."

"Smilloux. Their name is Smilloux. And my grandfather's name is Bartel. Etienne Bartel. Not The Pisser. Please remember that if you see them again."

"And your name is Joan. I'll remember that, too."

"If we don't meet again, remember that I don't hate you. I love you. I love you like a brother."

"You'll never know how good that makes me feel."

***

Poindex was as good as his word. Sweat was dripping from his Dali beard, but the ordnance was loaded, there was a smoke bomb just behind the cockpit, and I didn't have to look to know that a bottle of his best wine and a chunk of his very best cheese were secure in the cockpit. I gave him a hug. "It is people like you that make this war even slightly bearable and probably winnable. It is people like me that make it possible. Me and all the fools who made a war just because they could."

He stroked that sweaty beard. "I don't care about all the other fools. Just the fool I know, who is going to take on von Richthofen just because he can. I know I can't talk you out of it, and it's bad luck to say 'good luck.' So just go. I'll have supper for you no matter how late you return."

"Until then, have Perrier play a little tune for the girls. Keep them cheery. Later, my friend."

I remember him as a statue, unmoving as I taxied out onto the pasture. Then, just before I ran up the engine for takeoff, he waved. I saluted my usual silly salute. I've said so many goodbyes with silly salutes or hesitant waves. Only a few people have left indelible farewell images. Poindex, standing next to a cow turd with a look of resignation on his face, was one of them.

***

I flew a little faster than cruising. I had a long way to go, and I needed most of the travel to happen before dark. When I got to the part of the front closest to St. Chalon, I immediately went to work. I dove down just behind the German lines and began strafing, being careful not to hit anything. I saw a few muzzles flashes, so I knew I was being fired upon. That's what I had hoped for. I kept looking above for signs of aircraft, but the skies were empty. I made a hundred and eighty degree turn in the form of a chandelle and dive, and strafed some more. There were more muzzle flashes. Still no one but me in the sky. Back for one last pass. It might have been my imagination, but I could swear that everyone in the German army was shooting at me. There were still no aircraft in sight.

I pulled up just a little, pulled the throttle back and forth a few times, groped for the cord connected to the smoke bomb pin, pulled it and worked the throttle again. There was plenty of light, the plane was very purple, and the smoke was streaming behind me. I waggled the wings a bit and kept her straight, letting her slowly drop. When I was sure I was just out of sight of the trenches, I pulled the levers on both bombs. The damn things trailed beneath me, of course, and I had drifted so low that I almost bombed myself. I was pretty sure that the men in the trenches I had just left behind would hear the explosions and see some smoke. Most likely at least one hundred German infantry men would claim it was he who shot down the Purple Duke.

It was what I had warned von Richthofen about, and it freed him from a pledge he was reluctant to make. He would surely validate the idea that it was ground fire that brought about my demise. They could search for my seared corpse after the war, if they still remembered the Purple Duke.

***

I set the power on cruise and headed across the top of the lowlands toward the British Isles. I calculated I would have enough petrol to make a loch in Scotland which I had selected based on two requirements: it was the deepest lake in all of Great Britain, with near vertical drops from shore to bottom, and it was close to Invereagle. It would cap my escape.

With the airplane trimmed up, I could rummage around in the cockpit. I opened the wine and unwrapped the cheese, then eating and drinking as if I were in a fine restaurant on a romantic assignation. I fumbled through my mental file to choose my glamorous companion. Nancy? No. Better forget her, and she me. Joan? No. There was never a romance there, although that woman taught me something about myself, and what I come to be. But, no. Zubeyde, the Egyptian Turk with the Persian eyes? No. She was probably the lover of Mustafa Kemal by now. Why would she be in a Parisian eatery with me? Maricela, my first wife? No. God, no. Let her rest in peace. Laura, the thief? Maybe. She was certainly beautiful. She knew the right things to say and the right things to do. Asha, my black African beauty. No. That would be a death with. I only remember once, of all the times we made love, that I didn't bleed afterward. I was never queasy about a little blood, but it was inappropriate to love making. I started to settle on Laura, when I remembered Molly, my very first love, from seventy or so years before. Molly, the red haired girl who was more woman than I was man. I loved her and I left her in Scotland to seek my fortune in California. I hadn't thought of her in a long time. Now, in that cockpit, she was with me, her wavy red hair tumbling freely, getting in the way of the controls. I offered her wine, took a sip with her. I offered her cheese, which became a rich truffle soufflé, and tasted it with her. I ran my hand over her smooth thighs as she sat on my lap. Scandalous behavior for such a fancy restaurant. She was so enchanting I almost didn't realize I was coasting into England, and should turn northwest.

***

It was dark when I arrived at Loch Morag. The moon painted it as a sliver of silver, with a few black dots for the islands. I wanted the west shore, which had the steepest drop to the bottom, so I dragged it once, flying low and slow. There were a few lights, and I would ditch my plane as close to them as possible. When I was suddenly upon the brink of my decision, I felt a very real pang in my gut. This plane, the best in the world, put together by the best aeronautical engineer in the world, painstakingly but with urgency, just for me, was going to the bottom of the deepest lake in the British Isles, perhaps never to be seen again. She had served me so well, made me the scourge of the German High Command, allowed me to defeat von Richthofen man to man, and I was drowning her, making her a sacrificial maiden to my own newly found morality. Poor Purple Beauty. Poor Leplombe.. As consolation I rationalized: she would be preserved in the cold, unsalty depths. He would always think she and I died in service to the cause. And I could carry my self-righteousness as baggage for the rest of my life.

Before I turned for the water landing run I had to prepare. I had no idea how she would ditch, so I had to be ready if she pitched inverted and I would up under her as she started to sink. I had put the money stash which I always carried, and which consisted of some pound notes and some gold coins, in a water proof pouch. I hung that around my neck, under my clothes. I undid all the buttons and stays on my clothes and removed my shoes. I wasn't an expert at the crawl, but I was certain I could make the couple of hundred meters to shore before hypothermia set in if I shed my clothes. Then I could make for the nearest dwelling.

I cheated on calculating my chances. Getting free of the airplane was a coin flip. Getting to shore was a coin flip. Finding shelter and warmth while I was still ambulatory was a coin flip. If I calculated this properly, my chances of making it safely were probably less than 10%. If I separated each out, like any given flip of a coin, it was 50-50. I hadn't come this far to settle for true odds. I needed my reliable luck to even the chance. It hadn't failed me so far. Oh, maybe once or twice, but the data was well in my favor. Never mind the obvious question: how many times can you cheat death? Superstition aside, there is no proper answer to that question. That I'm telling this story shows that I still don't know. Perhaps the last thing I ever think of will be a number. It doesn't matter that I won't be able to tell anybody. It will only apply to me, anyway.

These are thoughts that ran through my mind as I prepared to plop the Purple Plane into Loch Morag and strip down to my one piece underwear. I turned and headed for the spot I had picked. I was pretty sure I wouldn't travel far once the wheels hit the water, even if they broke off. It would be a fight to keep from pitching over. If the bottom wings dug in they should produce enough downward force to counter-balance the weight of the engine. Maybe. Maybe. Maybe. I had to be ready for the worst outcome. I cut the engine. The bridge was burned down.

When I relive the scene, it is always in slow motion. I was gliding just above stall, down, the smooth water giving no good indication of altitude, down, wondering if I would ever touch, if I had died in the crash and there really was a hell, and I was doomed forever to hold Purple Beauty just off Loch Morag, begging Leplombe to forgive me. And then we touched.

She started to pitch, but when she did, water rushing over the lower wings held her down. It only added to my sorrow that Purple's last trip for me was as a boat, and she wasn't a boat for long. The holes in the fuselage let in water immediately, the torn wings were no help, and the engine was too heavy. I just had time to throw myself overboard and clear the struts, and she was gone. She's still there, a thousand feet down, undiscovered by even those who go looking for Lake Monsters in Scotland with modern equipment.

I started to swim immediately. Although I kept myself in good physical condition, I was a novice swimmer. I knew the crawl was the fastest way to get anyplace, and I had tried it a few times. Now, it was a necessity. I needed to get out of that water, and there was two to three hundred meters between me and land. There was no question whether I could swim that far as fast as I must. There was only the must.

I didn't get far before I realized that my underwear was doing nothing to retain body heat but doing a lot to increase drag. A pilot knows that drag fights efficiency, and I couldn't afford any decrease in efficiency. I would have to go beyond my limits as it was. The underwear had to go. I was down to my socks and my money pouch, and I was throwing my arms ahead and pulling them back as if I knew what I was doing. I had read something about kicking so I did that, too. At a summer swim party I would have seemed the fool. In that dark, cold lake I was proceeding slowly to land, and generating some heat while I did so. I was glad I had had that romantic dinner with Molly. I needed the fuel.

Even with the wine and cheese and the vigorous exercise, I could feel the cold eating at me. I would take twenty strokes and look up, twenty more. The dim light on the shore didn't seem closer. I began to doubt my estimate of the distance. I began to doubt my stamina. I began to think that I might have built a fatal error into this exploit. I began to argue with myself. *Are you afraid to die? No. Do you want to? No. Will you give up and just say fuck it? No. What if you can't make it? Then I can't make it. That has to be proven to me. Did you make some mistakes here? Yes. It's hard to judge distances at night. I should have run right up to the shore before I ditched. Then I could have kept my clothes. Maybe set fire to the plane. No. Pushed it into the loch. Why didn't you? Because I wanted to be sure it disappeared. It had to go down in a deep spot. I would have had to swim out here anyway, dragging an airplane. Who does that? You're an idiot either way. I know that.*

When I looked up after the argument the shore was much closer. I grunted against the shivers and I cashed in what energy I had left. I stroked harder and took forty strokes before I looked up again. I was glad I hadn't gone for a hundred. I had cocked off to the left. I might have begun to swim in circles. I took ten hard strokes toward the beach and looked. Maybe fifty feet left. I went for it.

I was almost arm's length from the shore before I could touch bottom. When I felt it at last, I made my legs do all the work hoisting me from the loch. As I paused on the little strip the natives there would call a beach, I realized I was shivering. My teeth would have chattered if I hadn't clenched my jaws. I knew I had to keep moving, trying to find a house, a person, with a fire. And maybe some clothes, though I could only think of fire.

The shore was rugged, with hills running down to the loch, broken by some gullies and creek beds. I had swum toward a light, so there had to be a dwelling up the gully where I coasted in. I scrambled over the cobbles and rough ground, my feet protected only by my wet socks. While swimming I had achieved a breathing rhythm. This half-running required a different rhythm, so I was soon panting, and I couldn't seem to get that 'second wind' again. I didn't care. I was going to arrive at someone's door, a wet, breathless, naked mad man, clad only in socks and a magic amulet. I started to laugh at myself. Me, the Purple Duke, terror of the skies, bane of the German High Command, buck ass naked, freezing, and running around in the Scotch woods like a man raised by wolves. Had I come down in the world? In fact. I felt free. Free of war and killing. And rather stupid. There had to be a better way to do this. Why hadn't I thought of it?

***

When the door to the rustic cottage opened she had the light at her back, so all I could see was the silhouette of a woman, and the only detail I could make out was her wavy red hair, tumbling to her shoulders. She was certainly a cool one. Her first words were, "Are you angel or devil?"

Chapter Sixteen

Somewhere in Time

Down among the sheltering pines

Fast to the forest floor

Deep in the dust of a million past lives

Lost in the silent roar

Now does a lone soul wander

Seeking it knows not what

It moves as a shadow of nothing

It lies like dirt in a rut

There must to something to reach for

There must be a reason in being

And yet when the soul thinks about it

There's something it just isn't seeing

So at last it blows out the candle

And leaves the key in the lock

The soul that once was so airy

Is now as hard as a rock

From the Rock Opera *Mary Was Out All Night, So I Took Jesus Fishing,* by Mencarlo Gianotti. The premier performance was in 1987, at the Escondido, California High School gymnasium. The school drama club provided extras (mostly playing fish) for the San Diego Theater Arts Company. The opera moved to San Diego, where it ran for three seasons, each season under a different name. It finally wound up with the title *Help Me, Help Me Wanda, Help Me Get It Out of My Mind.*

***

Without further word she led me by an arm into her house, through the living/kitchen area, and into a small bedroom. I followed, almost too exhausted to walk unaided. The entry area had been awash in light, with two kerosene lanterns, one in the window and one over the mantle turned up bright. The bedroom, however, was dimmer, with a single lantern turned lower. The bed, with a down cover, beckoned a man who was beyond his limits in fatigue. I let her guide me into the bed and cover me with the comforter. She could have killed me if she wished – I was so weakened. Yet, when she bent over me to adjust the cover, I knew she wouldn't, for I got my first good look at her face. It matched the seventy year old image of Molly, my first love and my cockpit dinner companion for the trip across the English Channel. With that confusing image I slipped into sleep.

***

When I awoke the light outside spoke of dawn. Or dusk. I didn't know which. My muscles were stiff and my feet were sore. Without looking, I could tell my socks were gone. I grabbed at my chest and found the pouch still there. It was my only item of dress. The image of the woman who dragged me in like a wet alley cat floated across my mind. A rattling from the other room in the cottage signaled someone's presence. Hers? There were things I needed to know, but I didn't want to approach her again stark naked. Being a nude stranger at a woman's door was bizarre enough done

229

once. She didn't need me prancing around like that again, although she knew me somewhat better than I knew her, given that I couldn't recall her ever being less than completely dressed. It would be easier just to call out.

"Hello," I yelled. "Red-haired woman? Hello?" I waited.

She appeared at the door. "I thought you'd sleep for two days," she said. "You never even noticed me sleeping beside you."

"What time is it?"

"Nearly supper time. You've been asleep for eighteen hours or so."

Dusk. Not dawn. How would I start a conversation with a woman I had met under such awkward circumstances, hadn't really met at all. It was more like an invasion. And she had been so kind. So far. "First, Miss.....?"

"Molly."

"I don't believe it."

"Why would I lie?"

"No, I mean....such a coincidence. I once knew a Molly. She looked quite a bit like you."

"They say I take after my grandmother, and so I'm named after her. I don't think you would know her, though. Looking at you, I'd say you were twenty years my junior. My grandmother died before you were born, I'd guess."

I was suddenly very sad, although I couldn't let it show. This could be some sort of predestined event, some karmic event, although I didn't believe in either. If this Molly was truly of early Molly's lineage, I didn't want to know. I was only interested in the existential. I had barged in on this Molly, she hadn't attacked me with an axe, she hadn't gone screaming in panic, she had just thrown my bare ass into bed, which was exactly my then immediate need. She was still calm and collected, doing her everyday chores, and talking quietly to a person who might well be crazy. So I started over. "First, let me thank you for your kindness. I had had a long, hard day and part of a night, I was nearly frozen, I hadn't had much to eat all day (and part of a night), and I came pounding on your door, unclothed and wild-eyed. You let me in and put me in a warm bed. I can't thank you enough. Oh, and you took off my wet socks."

"They weren't doing you any good, and I didn't want the bed to have any extra dampness." She was looking at me with a palpable tenderness. Did I notice a bit mischief around the eyes?

"Well, you did a lot for a desperate man. I'm still amazed that you didn't even hesitate. How did you know I wasn't a madman, or some sex fiend?"

"Do you remember my first words?"

They came to me immediately and clearly. "Was I angel or devil. Why did those things pop into your mind when a man in nothing but wet socks showed up at your door in the middle of the night?"

"Because I had prayed for either, and when I heard your airplane over the loch, and then the engine stop, I knew my prayers were answered. That's why I put the bright light in the window."

I couldn't help but laugh. "So, I came out of the sky in answer to the prayers of a pretty, lonely woman."

"Exactly."

"And am I angel or devil? Have you decided?"

"No. I don't care, although I would prefer the latter. More interesting, and more likely to do a lady a favor." When she said this she was pulling off the comforter. As I grabbed for it she said, "Don't worry, you'll get it back. And more." With that, her clothes were being shed. I've said it a hundred times, and I'll say it again. It amazing how fast a woman can undress when she wants to. When she was as naked as I she

232

said, "There. Time to get very warm." She climbed onto the bed beside me and pulled up the covers.

I guessed, before she told me, that she had not had conjugal relations for some time. She was rusty, but her appetite was huge. In fact, after a couple of hours I had to remind her that I was still in a weakened condition.

She rolled off me and sighed. "I'm sorry." She was stroking my face. "I kept my desires under control while you slept so long. I could see you needed it. When you finally woke up, I wanted too much, too soon." She sighed. "But I'm not ready to call it finished just yet. I hope you're not. I'll give you a little rest." She put her head back on her pillow. "Besides, I'd really like to know more about the first lover I've had in nearly ten years. I've been waiting for you, and I don't even know who I've been waiting for. What's your name? What sort of devil are you?"

"My name is Damon Maxwell. I'm a Scotch devil, although it's been a long time since I've been in Scotland." I stopped for a moment, trying to decide what sort of story I could fabricate. It had to have some elements of truth, along with my usual carefully crafted lies. "And yes, I'm a devil. I come to you straight from Hell. It's located someplace in Belgium, with a bunch of Germans on one side and a bunch of Frenchmen and Englishmen on the other. This devil was right in the middle."

Her smile was replaced by a frown. "I know of that hell. My son is there with the Black Guard. My only serious prayers are for him, that I see him again in one piece, vertical, and back here to stay."

I hadn't thought about the obvious. She was living by the side of Loch Morag alone. "Where is your son's father," I asked, although I already knew the answer.

"Dead. Nearly ten years. The boy and I could keep the place going. A few sheep, some crops in the ground fertilized with kelp. Now I do it all myself, although some men neighbors come around to help from time to time."

"No lovers among them."

That brought the smile back. "Their wives come with them. Or they send their brats along as chaperones. Any decent single men have gone. At least to Inverness, if not to Glasgow or Edinburgh." The smile became more tender. She touched my genitals. "And then these came falling from the sky."

"Why do you stay here? I know this was once a thriving place, but now....."

"Where would I go? I have little money and no skills that anyone would want. This is what I know."

I guessed her age at about fifty. Her hands were work hands and her face had seen some weather, but her body was supple from hard work and her physique thoroughly feminine. All in all, she was a handsome woman, and I told her so.

"So, handsome gets me what? I could go be a woman of the night? Go from one man in ten years to five men a day? A washwoman? I do that here. What's there for me anywhere? No, the world came to me when you fell to earth. Or came up from below." She considered. 'But, we were going to talk about you."

"What about me?"

She made a snorting laugh. "What about you? You must be joking. You come naked to my door, almost dead. Where did you come from? How did you get here? Why?"

"I told you. I was at the front. In the thick of it. I decided my job was done, and flew my airplane here. I ran out of gas over the loch and decided that was the safest place to put her down in the dark. I was farther from shore that I thought, and she sank like a rock. I had to swim for it, and my clothes were too much of a drag. I wouldn't have made it with them holding me back. I dragged myself up on shore. I thought I had seen a light up this gully before I crashed, so I headed this way. I finally saw your light in the window, the light you put there you say because you heard me buzzing around. That worked, apparently for both of us."

"I don't understand. You were at war, for the Royal Flying Service I guess. Do you people get to decide when you've done all the duty required and just leave when you feel like it? And go where you wish without telling anybody?"

"It was a special mission, with a certain desired outcome. I was approached by the Air Service as the most likely to carry it out. I was never really in the Air Service. And they have other duties for me. I can't tell you more than that." *At least not without lying even more than I have.*

She sat thinking a moment. Then, "I was going to commend you for your service. So I suppose I should, even though I don't know what it was. Still, I'm grateful to you flyers."

"Why is that?"

"I just had a letter from my son. He said a particular flyer probably saved his life. On a day when the Germans started an attack, a purple airplane appeared and spurted so much fire in that sector they had to fall back. Then, the next day, they had been ordered to go over the top, and attack the German trenches. He was sure they would all be killed by machine gunners, but just as they started the charge the same purple airplane showed up and shot up the Germans so badly that our boys suffered very few casualties, and they captured the trenches easily. Of course, they gave them back to German reinforcements two days later. Still, he thinks he's alive thanks to that purple airplane."

I didn't know what to say, so I covered it with the brainless remark, "That's remarkable."

"Do you know anything of the purple plane? Are there more than one? Why don't we leave the fighting of the war to such people and weapons?"

That was a good question, and it angered me. I thought I had freed myself from the mayhem, leaving it to the fools who started it. Now she reminded me: one might have a great repugnance for murder, but killing can and does save lives. It should be done by people like me, who have the constitution for it, even when we're fed up. I had sworn I would never go to another war. Now I was vacillating about going back to this one. What could I say to this Molly, whose son I had saved at least temporarily? Could I tell her *hey that was me but I'm not going back to keep doing it?* No. I had made my bed, at least for that war. And I was lying in hers. "Well, I'm glad your son is safe so far. I can't tell you much about purple airplanes, though. They do sound like the wrath of God, at least as far as the Germans are concerned. You're right. There should be more of them. I'm sure they take special pilots. I probably couldn't qualify. I found being shot at discomfiting."

"Well," she said, "I didn't pray for a hero. And I got my devil." With that she decided my rest period was over.

***

I was wearing her long dead husband's clothes. They almost fit. She had fetched them from a dusty trunk and they smelled as if they had been in there for the ten years she had mentioned. Clean, but musty. I took a bite of the breakfast-at-supper or supper-for-breakfast, whatever one might call it. It was some sort of sausage, warmed over biscuits with a bit of jam, and a native tea. I didn't know how hungry I was until I mouthed that first bite. I ate politely, but I ate everything. She watched all this with a smile, and waited until I was finished to begin the obvious conversation. "Putting my fantasy aside," she said, "I know you didn't fly from the battle field and plunge your airplane into the loch just to see me. So, where is it you're going, or do you know?"

I stretched back into my chair. "Oh, I know where I'm headed, but perhaps it wasn't chance that brought me here. Or, it was, at that. My usual *bon chance*. It all has me thinking. I needed you to literally save me from dying in the woods, which I was close to lying down and doing. And you needed someone to drop into your lonely life. So, let me tell you where I'm going, and then let me tell you an idea I have." She nodded, so I continued. "I have a fairly successful business in

Invereagle. A good friend manages it for me. I'm on my way there to see if he needs any input from me, and to gather some funds for further travel. I may be mistaken, but I think you would fit in someplace in the business. And I'm sure your son could find a place there, too. If he wished. I rather think he would like it. How will you convince him to toil his life away on this tiny farm after he's been abroad?"

She looked at me with a twist of her head and puzzled eyes. "You really are the devil. You come to me out of the night, make love to me, ply me with thoughts of a better life, tell me I'm handsome, and me old enough to be your mother." She shook her head, but her eyes never left mine, trying to penetrate my soul.

Her words slammed me like a fist atop my head. *Old enough to be your mother.* I winced even more at *make love to me.* I hadn't thought her likeness to Molly through, hadn't counted the years, inspected the chronology. For I might have answered *or old enough to be your grandfather.* The Molly of my youth and I knew nothing of contraceptives. And I had left so abruptly, never to communicate. The implications, however remote, were somewhat discomforting. However, what was done was done. Now I felt an even greater obligation to this woman. I cleared my throat. "I made love to you because you *are* a desirable woman. You owe it to yourself, and to your son, to consider my proposal. At least come with me to Invereagle and see what it's like. If you are favorably impressed, write a letter to your son. My guess is he will agree, and it will give him something to live for, to come back to, when this stupidity is over."

Her face hardened. "You call it 'stupidity.' Yet he very well may die for that stupidity, die in a place you just flew away from because you just decided to. How should I feel if he dies for nothing? Why do you deny his purpose? You say you are Scottish. Have you no patriotism, no antagonism toward the Kaiser? No love of country?"

What could I say? I was used to lying, but I was at a place where I couldn't override my real beliefs. "I have no devotion to any country. I haven't, for a very long time. I care about people, one at a time. That's all I can do. I care about you and your son at this moment. I hope he lives through this. And if he does, I hope you and he will find a better life through my offer."

"Then go save him. Fly him out as you flew yourself out."

"You know I can't do that. I no longer have access to an airplane, and even if I could, you wouldn't want me to make your son a deserter. You see, that's part of the stupidity. Even if someone high up would admit that the men in the trenches are just pawns in a chess game that has no good ending, they have their rules. If a pawn tries to leave before he is killed, he will be tracked down and killed. Once the game is started, there is no quitting, at least not by the pieces in the game. Only the King gets to say it's won or lost. I happen to believe the Kaiser will be checkmated, but not before many more pawns die. I hope your son isn't one of them. I truly care. I can honestly say I care as much as the pilot of the purple airplane who may have saved your son's life."

Her face softened. "I believe you do." She sighed and dropped her head to a hand. It was obvious her thoughts were ricocheting between options and outcomes. Perhaps she was praying, although I had noticed no religious icons in the cottage. Finally, she said, "There isn't that much I need to do here. I see no harm in accompanying you to Invereagle. I know you have means to buy us passage." She nodded at the pouch still hung around my neck.

I had to laugh. "I was at your mercy, and you showed much of it. That, and grace. It would be a honor to have your company on a trip to Invereagle."

Denis De Luchi

Chapter Seventeen

Whither Thou Goest

Aye, Cap'n

On the horizon

I see yonder black mass

Aye, Cap'n

I'll stand by ye

I'll hold that cyclone two points to the starboard

You and me, Cap'n

You send the boys aloft

I'll steady the rudder

It always like this, Cap'n

The sea, the wind, the snarl of the beast

We stand firm

And we face it

We live or we die

But we never run before the wind

For us, there's no place to run

You and me, Cap'n

One more time

There are two opinions as to the origin of this verse. The first concerns a jilted Bedouin lover who rode off into the Sahara, was thrown by his camel into a very fluid sand dune, and uttered these last words as he drowned. The second also involves a desert, this time the Atacama. A group of pre-Incan rafters, after drifting across the Pacific circa 30,000 BCE, finally landed in what is now Chile. The verse is said to have been found scratched on the chest of a mummy. It is claimed the discoverer was Teddy Roosevelt.

***

The trip to Invereagle was actually pleasant. It turned out that Molly, for all her years of hermitage, had lost none of her humanity. She was charming and a reasonably good conversationalist. She sensed my hesitancy to talk about things of the modern world, things like war and politics and industry. She assured me that the village near her cottage had radio receivers and even a weekly news bulletin. The locals swapped books and gossip, everyone was literate, and a few even had carefully formed, if crudely analytical, thoughts. The worldly IQ was probably higher than in the average metropolitan area, let alone farming community. We got along, and would have continued so, even if the journey had been much longer.

As it was, my magic amulet, or the gold therein, smoothed and otherwise facilitated the way for us. My only disquieting thoughts concerned my possible place in Molly's ancestry. Even as we conversed I argued with myself. Is it tolerable to make love to your granddaughter if she is fiftyish and you appear to be younger than thirty? If you are ignorant of a genetic link? If you are have half crazed from exposure and a thirty hour day full of combat, several demanding flights, near starvation, strong wine, all ending in an airplane crash and a naked swim in a Scottish loch? If you have lived so hard for so long that time has no meaning, if you are merely a symbol of the past, a ghost passing through generations with no real place to go? If you believe you have never sired a child, can't even remember all the women you have loved? Truly loved. For the most part. How about that peasant maid who met you outside that monastery in Greece? The one you literally tumbled in the hay with, the one who almost sapped all your strength, strength you needed to rescale that damn wall that faced two hundred feet above the Mediterranean Sea. Did she ever have child born of a wayward monk? *Stop it! You don't know. You'll never know. And Molly is too old to get pregnant. I think. And I'm pretty sure she's not my granddaughter, anyway.* I wondered why Rodrigo Rodriguez, the ancestor who told me about our curse, never warned me about this possibility. Did he never run across such a situation? I had decided I had better stay out of Scotland, just to be statistically safe.

So I looked at Molly and said to myself, "No, she's not related. She certainly didn't inherit the immortality gene if she is. I finally decided to let it go and just enjoy the company of this charming woman.

I wanted to make for her and her son a happier life. There are always problems with that type of kindness. First, it really isn't up to you to decide what makes another person happy. Second, if you don't believe the first, you have to be a great persuader. I have never been a good salesman, I suppose because I do believe the first. So I had to let Molly decide for herself. I knew her son would prefer Invereagle and an important job to a piss-ant farm and cottage beside Loch Morag. If he lived. If he didn't I couldn't predict what Molly would do.

I was going to leave the salesmanship up to Milos Stanic, my Serbian friend who was part of my Secret Police force in Serbia, acting on behalf of the Habsburgs. We were lucky to escape with our lives when the operation went south, but I had convinced Milos he could run my distillery in Invereagle while I banged out, doing whatever foolish things I was prone to do. I didn't know, until Molly and I arrived at Invereagle, how wise I was in picking Milos to be my distillery manager.

Without a word to me, since he never really knew where I was or what I was doing, using in part the generous salary I had suggested he pay himself and in part company profits, he had started two new enterprises. They were half owned by him and half owned by me, my half coming as a complete surprise to me. Milos had raised himself on the streets of Balkan cities, and he knew how to provide salable products, products of any sort, from selling *sjtakos* (a Balkan spicy pretzel) on the streets of Sarajevo to fencing gems on the streets of Belgrade. For me he had run the distillery better than any previous manager, started a fine woolen mill to supply the tailors of Saville Row, and created a precision machine shop to make parts for the new high demand item, generators. From all this he put a lot of money in the bank for me. Perhaps I had saved his life. He had certainly made me even richer than I already was, something I didn't know until I arrived, unannounced, at his office.

Molly and I had gone straight to that office. I asked her to wait in the foyer while I found Milos. Of course he was surprised, and so happy to see me alive I couldn't stop him talking. After he finally told me about all the grand business accomplishments, my first words were about Molly. "There is someone I want you to meet. She literally saved my life. I will tell you all about that later. For now, I want you to be friendly to her. She has had a hard life and deserves a better one now. I am hoping to get her to move from Loch Morag to Invereagle. Perhaps into a position in one of our new companies. And she has a son, currently at the front. If he lives, I am sure he would want to leave that poor farm and find better work. You know I'm not a good persuader, except by violence or threat thereof. You are better suited to cajole a woman into a life change. Will you do that for me?"

Milos stroked his narrow nose, appropriate to his narrow face and generally narrow body. People might think him a slight man, and some miserable fools had made the mistake of taking him lightly. He was, in fact, all leather and muscle. And full of integrity, which is interesting for a man who had been, like me, an assassin, among other dark callings. Sensing my emotional connection to Molly, he simply said, "Let's go meet this Molly. If anyone can persuade her to move to Invereagle, I can."

Milos had learned a decent amount of Scottish Gaelic, so he immediately charmed Molly. I had been introduced to that language as a schoolboy, and then immediately forgotten it when I went out into the world. I let them speak to each other without interruption for a long while. I knew he was selling her on coming to work in Invereagle, and I wanted to stay out of his way.

***

I didn't remain in Invereagle long, just long enough to see Molly wavering. Since I had little interest in business beyond the ace-in-the-hole large bank account, I didn't want to peer over Milos' shoulder. He could persuade Molly, and he could run what was becoming an empire better than I ever could. My muscles were aching for a counterforce, my mind aching for a challenge. My renewed workouts in the spiritual and physical vigor of the Eastern martial arts only exaggerated these aches. I was ready to search for new adventure, a fact which announced to Milos and Molly abruptly, the day before my departure for America. I was in Invereagle barely three weeks.

***

I hadn't decided where I wanted to next abide, so I trained down to Glasgow and took a hotel room on a weekly basis. I didn't know if I could wait out the war, even when America decided to repay their debt to Lafayette. Still, I just couldn't decide where there would be mutual satisfaction in my residence. It became apparent that I couldn't stay in Glasgow interminably. I never really liked the place that much.

Then I thought of my place of meditation after a harrowing adventure in Southern Africa – the monastery at Phulminastes. I could never go back to the monastery, but I could go back to the town of Lavronikita, on the island of Chalcidique. It was a quiet place, removed from the war, a place where I could think and plan. And enjoy the sea. And maybe find that old sweetheart. I just needed to get there, which I accomplished by booking passage on a cargo ship running a Portuguese flag. That got me as far as Patra, and the rest was easy.

***

I had a few communications with Milos after the war but before I left Lavronikita. Molly did in fact move to Invereagle, as did her son, and they both found work in the Stanos/Maxwell Business Empire. Many of the boys returning from the trenches told the same story Molly's son did – of a Purple Avenging Angel that appeared over the lines from time to time, harassing the Germans and saving Allied lives. A few saw this angel crash one day, bringing tears to the eyes of grown men. No wreckage was ever found, and the British Command was not forthcoming as to the identity of the pilot or the origin of the airplane. I'm pretty sure my Purple Beauty will sit at the bottom of Loch Morag forever undiscovered. Morag doesn't have a notorious monster like Loch Ness, so no busybody will waste time with expensive sonar equipment scouring its bottom.

One last note. Not long after my final encounter with von Richthofen, he received a fatal wound while engaged in aerial combat. He actually landed the aircraft safely, but died, I believe, in the cockpit. The kill was credited to a British pilot, but controversy began almost immediately. The trajectory of the bullet was from below and to the right, when the British pilot was above and to the left. This led most experts to conclude von Richthofen was killed by ground fire.

I told him so.

Denis De Luchi

Made in the USA
San Bernardino, CA
17 May 2014